MT. LOGAN MIDDLE SCHOOL
MEDIA CENTER

W9-BFJ-416

RETOLD TALES SERIES

RETOLD AMERICAN CLASSICS
VOLUME 1

RETOLD AMERICAN CLASSICS
VOLUME 2

RETOLD BRITISH CLASSICS

RETOLD WORLD CLASSICS

The Perfection Form Company, Logan, Iowa 51546

CONTRIBUTING WRITERS

Michael A. Benware
B.A. English
English Teacher

Robert A. Klimowski
M.A. Reading, B.A. English
English Teacher

Beth Obermiller
M.A. English
Educational Writer

Michele Price
B.A. Communications
Educational Writer

Rebecca Schwartz
M.A. English
English Teacher

Kristen L. Wagner
B.A. English
English Teacher

Mary J. Wagner
M.S. Reading, B.A. English
Reading Coordinator

FIELD TESTERS

Ken Holmes
Lincoln High School
East St. Louis, Illinois

Robert A. Klimowski
Weeks Transitional School
Des Moines, Iowa

Dawn McDuffie
Mumford High School
Detroit, Michigan

Michal Reed
Bartlett Junior High School
Springville, California

RETOLD TALES SERIES

RETOLD
WORLD
CLASSICS

R
808.83
Mye

79077

1990
$10.95

DISCARD MT. LOGAN MIDDLE SCHOOL
MEDIA CENTER

THE PERFECTION FORM COMPANY

Editors:
Kathy Myers
Beth Obermiller

Cover Art: Craig Bissell
Book Design: Craig Bissell & Dennis Clark
Inside Illustration: Tim Earp

Copyright 1987. The Perfection Form Company, Logan,
Iowa. All rights reserved. No part of this book may
be used or reproduced in any manner whatsoever
without written permission from the publisher.

TABLE
OF CONTENTS

THE VOYAGES OF SINDBAD THE SAILOR
from *The Arabian Nights*   **1**

THE BET
Anton Chekhov   **31**

THE NIGHTINGALE
Hans Christian Andersen   **45**

GOD SEES THE TRUTH, BUT WAITS
Leo Tolstoy   **61**

A PIECE OF STRING
Guy de Maupassant   **77**

THE DIARY OF A MADMAN
Nikolai Gogol   **91**

THE NECKLACE
Guy de Maupassant   **127**

THE BISHOP'S CANDLESTICKS
Victor Hugo   **143**

WELCOME TO THE RETOLD WORLD CLASSICS

The turban from the Mideast, champagne from France, and caviar and *The Nutcracker Suite* from Russia. What do this piece of clothing, drink, appetizer, and ballet have in common? They're all great world classics.

We call something a classic when it is so well loved that it is saved and passed down to new generations. Classics have been around for a long time, but they're not dusty or out of date. That's because they are brought back to life by each new person who sees and enjoys them.

The *Retold World Classics* are stories written years ago that continue to entertain or influence today. The tales offer exciting plots, important themes, fascinating characters, and powerful language. They are stories that many people have loved to hear and share with one another.

RETOLD UPDATE

This book presents a collection of eight adapted classics. All the colorful, gripping, or comic details of the original stories are here. But, in the Retold translations of the stories, long sentences and paragraphs have been split up. And some old words have been replaced with modern language.

In addition, a word list has been added at the beginning of each story to make reading easier. Each word defined on that list is printed in dark type within the story. If you forget a word while you're reading, just check the list to review the definition.

You'll also see footnotes at the bottom of some story pages. These notes identify people or places, explain ideas, or even let you in on an author's joke.

Finally, at the end of each tale you'll find a little information about the author. These revealing and sometimes amusing facts will give you insight into a writer's life and work.

When you read the Retold Tales, you bring each story back to life in today's world. We hope you'll discover why the Retold Tales have earned the right to be called World Classics.

THE VOYAGES OF SINDBAD THE SAILOR

FROM *THE ARABIAN NIGHTS*

VOCABULARY PREVIEW

Below is a list of words that appear in the story. Read the list and get to know the words before you start the story.

adhere—stick or cling to
allotted—allowed, gave out, or assigned
amassed—collected or stored up
bartering—trading or swapping
calamity—disaster; tragedy
confounded—puzzled; bewildered
crevice—a narrow crack or opening, especially in rock
decreed—ordered or commanded
dilate—expand or swell
diverting—turning aside; redirecting
extensive—wide in scope or amount; broad
girth—distance around
impaled—pierced with a sharp object; speared
obsessed—completely taken over by the thought of
populous—filled with many people
realm—kingdom
requite—repay or reward
suffice—serve or suit; be enough
ventured—dared or risked
wane—fade or die away

THE VOYAGES OF SINDBAD THE SAILOR

FROM THE ARABIAN NIGHTS

Sindbad is a man who loves his comfort. Yet, time and again, he feels the pull of the sea and distant lands.

Perhaps his adventures on these voyages will cure him of his itch. That is *if* he can survive monstrous birds, cannibals, and a pit of living death.

Know, O my brothers, that I was living easily and in great happiness. My life was sheer delight. But then one day I became **obsessed** with the thought of traveling about the world and seeing other cities and islands. A longing seized me to trade and make a fortune.

Upon deciding this, I gathered a great sum of cash. Buying goods and gear fit for travel, I packed them up.

Then I went down to the riverbank. There I found a noble, brand-new ship ready to sail. It was equipped with sails of fine cloth and had a good crew and many supplies.

So I went aboard, with a number of other merchants. After loading our goods, we weighed anchor[1] the same day.

Our voyage was very pleasant. We sailed from place to place and from isle to isle. Whenever we anchored we met a crowd of merchants and important people and customers. We took to buying and selling and **bartering**.

At last destiny brought us to an island, fair and green. This isle was covered with fragrant flowers. There were trees bearing yellow-ripe fruits. Birds warbled soft tunes. Radiant, crystal-clear streams flowed.

But no sign of humans could be seen—not even a blower of the fire.

The captain anchored offshore this island. The merchants and sailors landed and walked about. They enjoyed the shade of the trees and the song of the birds that chanted the praises of the One, the Victorious.[2] In turn, the passengers and sailors marveled at the works of the Almighty King.

I landed with the rest. Sitting down by a spring of sweet water among the trees, I took out some food I had with me. I began eating that which Allah Almighty had **allotted** to me. So sweet was the breeze and so fragrant were the flowers that I soon felt drowsy. Lying down, I was quickly drowned in sleep.

When I awoke, I found myself alone. The ship had sailed and left me behind. Not one of the merchants or sailors had remembered me.

---

[1]To weigh anchor is to lift it out of the water. This frees a ship and allows it to set sail.

[2]"The One, the Victorious" is Allah. Allah is the Islamic term for God. Sindbad and his fellow travelers are Moslems.

I searched the island right and left but found neither man nor jinn.[3] The discovery upset me beyond words. I was nearly bursting with anguish and concern. Here I was, weary and heartbroken, left quite alone. I had no equipment or meat or drink.

So I gave myself up for lost and said, "Not always does a jug survive a fall. On my first voyage, I was saved by finding one who brought me from the desert island to an inhabited place.[4] But now there is no hope for me."

Then I fell to weeping and wailing and gave myself up to a fit of rage. I blamed myself for having again **ventured** upon a dangerous voyage, filled with perils. I had left the ease of my house in my own land, where the pleasures of good meat, drink, and clothing had been mine. I had lacked nothing, neither money nor goods.

And I repented of having left Baghdad. This regret was all the stronger because I had so narrowly escaped all my troubles and dangers in my first voyage. I exclaimed "Truly we are Allah's and back to Him we return!"

I was indeed just like a madman or one enchanted by a jinn.

After awhile, I rose and walked about the island. I wandered right and left and every which way. I was unable to sit or linger in any one place because I was so upset.

Then I climbed a tall tree and looked in all directions. I saw nothing except sky, sea, trees, birds, isles, and sands.

But after awhile, my eager glance fell upon some great white thing. It lay far off in the interior of the island. So I came down from the tree and walked towards that which I had seen.

Behold! It was a vast white dome rising high in the air. It was huge. I walked all around it but found no door. Nor

[3] A jinn is a spirit with supernatural powers. A jinn may be either friendly or hostile.
[4] Sindbad has made a voyage previous to this one. Altogether, he makes seven trips.

did I have enough strength or nimbleness to climb it. It was smooth and slippery and hard to hold on to.

So I marked the spot where I stood and went round about the dome to measure it. I found it was at least a good fifty paces around.

And as I stood, thinking about how to get inside the dome, behold! The sun was suddenly hidden and the air became dull and dark. The day was near its end and the sun just over the horizon. I thought a cloud must have passed over the sun.

But I marveled that a cloud would appear in the summertime.[5] Lifting my head, I looked steadily at the sky. I saw that the cloud was actually an enormous bird, of gigantic **girth** and incredibly wide wingspread. As it flew through the air, it veiled the sun and hid it from the island.

At this sight my wonder doubled. I recalled a story I had heard once from pilgrims and travelers. It was said that in a certain island lived a huge bird called the rukh, which fed its young on elephants. I was certain that the dome which caught my sight must be a rukh's egg.

I looked and wondered at the amazing works of the Almighty. Just then the bird landed on the dome. There it settled down. With its wings covering the egg, it stretched its legs out behind it on the ground. In this posture it fell asleep. Glory be to Him who does not sleep!

When I saw this, I arose. I unwound my turban from my head, then doubled it and twisted it into a rope. I tied one end to my middle and bound my waist fast to the legs of the rukh.

To myself I said, "Perhaps this bird will carry me to a land of cities and people. That will be better than staying on this desert island."

I passed the night watching and fearing to sleep, lest the bird should fly away with me when I was unprepared.

---

[5]Most regions in the Middle East have rain only during the winter.

At last the dawn broke and morning shone. Then the rukh rose off its egg. Spreading its wings with a great cry, it flew up into the air, dragging me with it. It did not cease to soar and climb till I thought it had reached the limit of the sky.

After that it descended earthwards. Finally it landed on the top of a high hill.

As soon as I found myself on the hard ground, I quickly untied myself. I shook for fear of the bird. But it took no heed of me nor even felt me. I unwound my turban from its feet and made off at my top speed.

Soon I saw the rukh grab something from the earth in its huge claws and rise with it high in the air. Peering more closely, I saw its prey was a gigantic serpent. The rukh flew away with the serpent clean out of sight.

I marveled at this and, going onwards, found myself on a peak overlooking a valley. This valley was very **extensive**, wide, and deep. It was surrounded by vast mountains that towered high in the air. None could see the tops of these peaks because of their dizzying height. Nor could anyone scale them.

When I saw this, I blamed myself for what I had done. I cried, "Would to Heaven that I had stayed on the island! It was better than this wild desert. There at least I had fruit to eat and water to drink. Here there are no trees, fruits, or streams.

"But there is no Majesty and there is no Might except in Allah, the Glorious, the Great! Truly, as often as I am out of one peril, I fall into a worse danger."

However, I took courage. Walking along the wadi,[6] I found that its soil was of diamond—the stone with which they pierce minerals. Precious stones and porcelain were also scattered there. And I saw onyx, which is a dense, hard

---

[6]A wadi is a type of dry stream bed found in Asia and Africa. Usually a wadi is filled with water only during the rainy season.

stone. Neither iron nor rock can scratch it; only with leadstone can it be broken or cut.

I also found that the valley swarmed with snakes and vipers. Each was big as a palm tree and could have swallowed an elephant in one gulp.

These serpents came out only by night. By day, they hid for fear the rukhs and eagles would pounce on them and tear them to pieces. This was the habit of the birds, though why they did it I do not know.

And I was sorry for what I had done. "By Allah, I have hurried to bring destruction upon myself!" I cried.

The day began to **wane** as I went along. I looked about for a place to sleep, being in fear of the serpents. I took no thought of meat or drink because I was so concerned for my life.

Soon I spotted a cave close by with a narrow doorway. I entered. Seeing a great stone, I rolled it up to the mouth of the cave and blocked the entrance.

I said to myself, "I am safe here for the night. As soon as it is day, I will go forth and see what destiny awaits me."

Then I looked to the back of the cave. There I saw a great serpent nesting with her eggs.

My flesh quaked and my hair stood on end. But I raised my eyes to Heaven and, leaving my destiny to fate, I stayed there all that night without sleep.

At daybreak I rolled back the stone from the mouth of the cave and came out. I staggered like a drunken man, dizzy from sleeplessness, fear, and hunger. In this pathetic condition I walked along the valley.

Behold! All at once there fell down before me a slaughtered beast. But I saw no one. I marveled with great marvel.

Then I remembered a story I had heard before from traders, pilgrims, and travelers. They told of how the mountains around the valley of diamonds are full of perils and terrors. No one dared to travel through them.

But the merchants who trade in diamonds have a way of getting the gems. These traders take a sheep and slaughter it. Then they skin the animal and cut it into pieces.

Taking the raw meat, they cast it from the mountaintops into the valley. Since the mutton is fresh and sticky with blood, some of the gems **adhere** to it.

There the merchants leave the meat till midday. At that time the eagles and vultures swoop down upon the meat and carry it in their claws to the mountain summits.

When they see this, the merchants come and shout at them, scaring them away from the meat. Then the men gather the diamonds which they find sticking to the mutton. They go their ways with the jewels and leave the meat to the birds and beasts. This is the only way to get the diamonds.

So, when I saw the slaughtered beast fall, I remembered the story. I went up to the beast. Into my pockets, thick belt, turban, and the folds of my clothes I loaded the choicest diamonds.

While I was doing this, down fell before me another great piece of meat. Then I lay down on my back and tied myself to the dead animal with my unrolled turban. When I was finished, my body was hidden under the dead beast.

Hardly had I settled myself when an eagle swooped down upon the mutton. Seizing it with his talons, he flew up with it high in the air, with me clinging underneath.

The bird did not stop flying until it landed on the peak of one of the mountains. There it dropped the meat and began tearing at it.

But, behold! There arose behind the bird a great shouting and clattering of wood. The bird was afraid and flew away.

Then I untied myself from the meat and stood up. My clothes were smeared with blood. At that moment the merchant ran up who had cried out at the eagle. Seeing me standing there, he was struck wordless with fear.

However, he soon went to the dead animal. Turning it over, he found no diamonds sticking to it.

At that he gave a great cry. He exclaimed, "Alas, my disappointment! There is no Majesty and there is no Might except in Allah. We seek refuge in Allah from Satan the damned!"

He moaned again and beat his hands together, saying, "Alas, the pity of it! How did this come about?"

Then I went up to him, and he said to me, "Who are you and what causes you to come here?"

And I replied, "Fear not. I am a man and a good one at that, as well as a merchant. My story is wondrous and my adventures are marvelous. The manner of my coming here is astonishing.

"So be of good cheer. You shall receive a delightful reward from me. I have with me plenty of diamonds, and I will give you as much as shall **suffice** you. Each of my gems is better than anything you could get by any other means. So fear nothing."

The man rejoiced when he heard that and thanked and blessed me. Then we talked till the other merchants, hearing me speaking to their companion, came up and greeted me. Each of them had also thrown down his piece of meat.

We all set off together. As we went, I told them my whole story. I related how I had suffered hardships at sea and the way I had reached the valley.

Then I gave the owner of the meat some of the stones I had with me. He was delighted and very thankful. He and all the merchants cheered my escape.

They said, "By Allah, a new life has been **decreed** for you. No one has ever reached that valley and come out of it alive before you. Praised be Allah for your safety!"

We passed the night in a safe and pleasant place. I stayed with them, rejoicing that I had escaped the valley of serpents and found an inhabited land.

On the next day we set out and journeyed over the mighty range of mountains. I saw many serpents in the valley.

Finally we came to a large, lovely island. There was a

garden of huge camphor trees.[7] Each tree could have shaded a hundred men.

When any of these people have a mind to get camphor, they bore into the upper part of the trunk with a long iron spike. Then the liquid camphor, which is the sap of the tree, flows out. They catch the camphor in vessels. The collected camphor soon sets like gum. But, after this, the tree dies and becomes firewood.

There is also on this island a kind of wild beast called a rhinoceros. It grazes like our steers and buffaloes. But it is a huge brute, bigger than the camel. And, like a camel, it feeds on leaves and twigs of trees.

This rhinoceros, or rhino, is a remarkable animal. It has a huge, thick horn—ten cubits[8] long—in the middle of its head. When cut in half, this horn looks like a man.

Voyagers and pilgrims and travelers say that this beast will carry off a great elephant on its horn. Then it will graze about the island and the seacoast, taking no heed of the elephant until the elephant dies.

After that, the elephant's fat melts in the sun and runs down into the rhino's eyes. This blinds the rhino, so that he is forced to lie down on the shore. Then comes the rukh bird and carries off both the rhino and the **impaled** elephant to feed its young.[9]

Besides these marvels, I also saw on this island many kinds of oxen and buffaloes. They were not like those found in our country.

On this island I sold some of the diamonds which I had and received gold and silver coins. I traded other gems for the produce of the country.

---

[7]Camphor trees are typically found in the Far East. They can be tapped for camphor, which is used in medicine, mothballs, etc.

[8]A cubit is an old-fashioned measurement. One cubit usually equals 18-21 inches.

[9]This passage is obviously pure fantasy.

Loading my goods upon beasts of burden, I journeyed on with the merchants from valley to valley and town to town. I traded as much as I could. And all the while I viewed the foreign countries and the works and creatures of Allah.

Finally we came to Al Basrah. We stayed there a few days, and then I resumed my journey to Baghdad.[10] I arrived at home with a great wealth of diamonds, money, and goods.

There I reunited with my friends and relations. I gave alms[11] and presented gifts to all my friends.

Then I settled down to eating and drinking well and wearing fine clothes and making merry with my friends. With light and happy heart, I forgot all my sufferings.

And everyone who heard of my return came and questioned me. They asked about my adventures in foreign countries. I told them all that had befallen me and what I had suffered. They marveled at my story and rejoiced with me at my safe return.

This, then, is the end of the story of my second voyage.

Know, O my brothers, that after I returned from my third voyage, I rejoined my friends.[12] I forgot all my perils and hardships in my new comfort and ease.

One day I was visited by a company of merchants. They sat down with me and talked of foreign travel and traffic.

Soon the old bad man within me yearned to go with them and enjoy the sight of strange countries. I longed for the society of the various races of mankind and for trade and profit.

So I resolved to travel with my visitors. I bought the

[10]Al Basrah and Baghdad are major cities in Iraq.

[11]Alms are gifts given to the poor. Giving alms is one of the religious duties of a Moslem.

[12]The tale of Sindbad's fourth voyage begins here. His third voyage has been omitted.

necessaries for a long voyage. I stored up a great supply of costly goods—more than ever before. Then I transported them from Baghdad to Al Basrah. There I boarded a ship with the merchants. They were the most important traders in town.

We set out, trusting in the blessing of Almighty Allah. With a favorable breeze and the best weather we sailed from island to island and sea to sea.

One day there arose against us a strong wind. The captain dropped anchor and brought the ship to a standstill. He was afraid his ship might be sunk in mid-ocean. Then we all fell to praying and humbling ourselves before the Most High.

But while we were doing this, a furious storm struck us. It tore the sails to rags and tatters. The anchor chain broke and the ship began to sink. We were cast into the sea, goods and all.

I kept myself afloat by swimming half the day. Finally, when I had given myself up for lost, the Almighty threw in my way one of the planks of the ship. I and some others of the merchants scrambled to reach it. Mounting it as we would a horse, we paddled with our feet in the sea.

We remained like this a day and a night, the wind and waves helping us on. On the second day, shortly before midmorning, the breeze and the sea stirred. The rising waves cast us upon an island. We were almost dead from fatigue, sleeplessness, cold, hunger, fear, and thirst.

We walked about the shore and found many herbs. We ate enough of these to keep breath in our bodies and lift our failing spirits. Then we lay down next to the sea and slept till morning.

When morning came with its gleam and shine, we arose and walked about the island to the right and left. At last we came in sight of a house far off.

We headed towards it and did not cease walking till we reached the door of it. Then lo! A number of naked men poured out from it. Without greeting us or saying a word, they seized us. Then they carried us to their King, who gestured for us to sit.

So we sat down, and they placed food before us. We did not recognize it and had never seen anything like it in all our lives.

My companions ate it because they were so hungry. But my stomach revolted from it and I would not eat.

My refusing it explains, by Allah's grace, why I am still alive. For no sooner had my comrades tasted it than their reason fled and their condition changed. They began to devour their food like madmen possessed by an evil spirit.

Then the savages gave them coconut oil to drink and they greased my friends with it too. As soon as they drank this, the merchants' eyes rolled back into their heads. They again fell to eating greedily in a most unnatural way.

When I saw this, I was **confounded** and concerned for them. Nor was I less anxious about myself, because I feared the naked folk.

So I watched the savages closely. It was not long before I discovered them to be a tribe of Magian[13] cannibals whose King was a ghoul.[14] Anyone who came to their country or whomever they caught in their valleys and on their roads they brought to their King.

Then the savages would feed the captives that strange food and grease them with oil. This caused their captives' stomachs to **dilate** so they could eat huge amounts.

Meanwhile, the captives lost their minds and the power of thought, becoming idiots. They were stuffed with coconut oil and food till they became fat and gross.

At that point the cannibals slaughtered the captives and roasted them for the King. But, as for the rest of the savages, they ate the flesh raw.

---

[13]The Magian were ancient priests of the Mideast. They were known for their magical powers.

[14]Ghouls are demons that eat corpses.

When I saw this, I was deeply dismayed for myself and my comrades. They had now become so dazed that they did not know what was being done to them. So the naked folk turned them over to a man who led them out every day and pastured them on the island like cattle. My friends wandered among the trees and rested at will, thus growing very fat.

As for me, I wasted away and became sickly out of fear and hunger. My flesh shriveled on my bones.

When the savages saw this, they left me alone and never thought of me. In fact, they forgot about me so entirely that one day I gave them the slip. Walking out of their country, I headed for the beach, which was distant.

At the beach, I spied a very old man seated on a hill encircled by water. I looked at him and recognized him. He was the herdsman who was in charge of pasturing my companions. With him were many others in the same situation as my friends.

As soon as he saw me, he knew I was sane and not like the rest whom he watched. So he waved to me from afar, as though he were saying, "Turn back and take the right-hand road. That will lead you to the King's highway."

So I turned back as he wanted me to and followed the right-hand road. As I went, I sometimes ran for fear. Other times I walked slowly to rest myself. I kept this up until I was out of the old man's sight.

By this time the sun had gone down and darkness had set in. So I sat down to rest. I would have slept, but sleep would not come to me that night. I was too distressed by fear and hunger and fatigue.

When the night was half over, I rose and walked on. Finally the day dawned in all its beauty. The sun rose over the heads of the lofty hills and across the low gravelly plains.

Now I was weary, hungry, and thirsty. So I ate my fill of herbs and grasses that grew in the island. In this way I kept life in my body and filled my stomach.

After that I set out again. I walked all that day and the

next night. I quieted my hunger with roots and herbs. I did not stop walking for seven days and seven nights.

On the morning of the eighth day, I caught sight of a faint object in the distance. So I made towards it, though my heart quaked for all I had suffered from first to last.

Behold! I discovered the object was a company of men gathering pepper.[15]

As soon as they saw me, they hastened up to me. Surrounding me on all sides, they said to me, "Who are you and where do you come from?"

I replied, "Know, O folk, that I am a poor stranger." Then I told them my story and all the hardships and perils I had suffered.

They marveled greatly at my tale and cheered my escape. They exclaimed, "By Allah, this is wonderful!

"But how did you escape from those savages who swarm in the island and devour all who fall into their hands? No one is safe from them and no one can get out of their clutches."

I told them the fate of my companions. Then they made me sit by them till they finished their work. They gave me some good food, which I ate, for I was hungry. I rested awhile, too.

After that they took me aboard their ship and carried me to their island home. There they brought me before their King, who returned my greeting. He received me honorably and questioned me about my history.

I told him all that had happened to me since the day I left Baghdad. He listened to my adventures with great wonder, he and his nobles, and told me to sit beside him.

When my tale was finished, he called for food. I dined with him and ate all my heart desired. Then I gave thanks to Almighty Allah for all His favors, praising and glorifying Him.

[15]Pepper grows in berry form on a shrub found in hot climates.

Afterwards I left the King and walked about the city to ease my mind. I discovered that it was wealthy and **populous**. I found many markets well-stocked with food and goods, filled with buyers and sellers.

So I rejoiced at having reached so pleasant a place. I settled there after my fatigues. I made friends with the townsfolk. It was not long before I became more honored and favored with the people and their King than any of the chief men of the **realm**.

Now I observed that all the citizens—great and low—rode fine, high-priced, thoroughbred horses. But they had no saddles or bridles.

I wondered at this and said to the King, "O my lord, why do you not ride with a saddle? A saddle increases a rider's comfort and control."

"What is a saddle?" he asked. "I never saw or used such a thing in all my life."

I answered, "With your permission, I will make you a saddle. That way you may ride on it and see how comfortable it is."

And he replied, "Do so."

So said I to him, "Furnish me with some wood." After it was brought, I sought out a clever carpenter. Sitting beside him, I showed him how to make the saddle, sketching the design of it in ink on the wood.

Then I took wool and turned it into felt. Covering the saddle with leather, I stuffed it and polished it. Then I attached the belly and stirrup straps. After that I fetched a blacksmith and explained the design of the stirrups and bridle bit.

So he forged a fine pair of stirrups and a bit and filed them smooth and coated them with tin. Meanwhile, I tied some silk fringes to the saddle and fitted leather to the bit.

Then I fetched one of the best of the royal horses. Saddling and bridling him, I hung the stirrups on the saddle and led the animal to the King. The outfit took his fancy and he thanked me. Then he mounted and rejoiced greatly in the saddle. He rewarded me handsomely for my work.

When the King's Wazir[16] saw the saddle, he asked me for one like it. So I made one for him. Furthermore, all the nobles and officers of state came to me for saddles.

So I began to make many saddles (having taught the craft to the carpenter and blacksmith). Selling them to all who wanted them, I **amassed** great wealth. I also stood in high honor and great favor with the King, his household, and nobles.

I lived like this for some time. Then one day, as I was sitting contentedly with the King, he turned to me. He said, "Know that you have become one of us, as dear as a brother. We hold you in such regard and affection that we cannot part with you or allow you to leave our city.

"Therefore I desire your obedience in a certain matter. I will not have you deny me."

I answered, "O King, what is it you desire of me? Far be it from me to deny you anything. I owe you many favors and much kindness. Praised be Allah, I am one of your humble servants."

He said, "I have a mind to marry you to a lovely, clever, and agreeable woman. And she is as wealthy as she is beautiful. In this way you will become a citizen and settle down with us. You will live with me in my palace. Please do not oppose me or cross me in this."

When I heard these words I was ashamed and held my peace. I could not even answer him because of my great bashfulness before him.

He asked, "Why do you not give me a reply, O my son?"

I answered, "O my master, your wish is my command, O king of the age!"

---

[16]A wazir (or vizier) is an important adviser to the ruler in certain Moslem countries.

So he summoned the Kazi[17] and the witnesses. Straightaway I was married to a lady of a noble family. She was wealthy in money and goods, the flower of an ancient family. She was also of great beauty and grace and the owner of farms, estates, and many a house.

Now after the King my master had married me to this wonderful wife, he also gave me a great and fine house. He staffed this with slaves and officers and gave me pay and allowances.

So I fell into complete ease and peace and delight. I forgot everything which had happened that had brought me weariness and hardship. For I loved my wife with the fondest love, and she loved me no less. We were as one and lived in the greatest comfort and happiness.

And I said to myself, "When I return to my native land, I will take her with me."

But whatever is destined for a man must occur. And no man knows what will happen to himself.

We lived in happiness a great while till Almighty Allah took the wife of one of my neighbors.

Now this neighbor was a friend of mine. So hearing the cry of the mourners, I went in to comfort him on his loss.

I found him in a very sad state, full of trouble and weary of soul and mind.

I sympathized with him and comforted him. I told him, "Do not mourn for your wife, who has now found the mercy of Allah. The Lord will surely give you a better one to fill her place, and your name shall be great and you shall live a long life!"

But he wept bitter tears and replied, "O my friend, how can I marry another wife? How shall Allah give me a better woman when I have but one day left to live?"

---

[17]A Kazi (or qadi) is a judge who interprets and oversees the religious laws of Moslems.

"O my brother," said I, "return to your senses. Do not announce the news of your own death. You are well, healthy, and comfortable."

"Upon your life, O my friend," he returned, "I swear that tomorrow you will lose me. And you will never see me again till the Day of Judgment."[18]

I asked, "How so?"

He answered, "This very day they bury my wife. They will also bury me with her in the same tomb.

"It is the custom with us that if the wife dies first, the husband will be buried alive with her. And in the same way with the wife if the husband dies first. This is so that neither may enjoy life after losing his or her mate."[19]

"By Allah," cried I, "this is a most horrid, disgusting custom. It should not be endured by anyone!"

Meanwhile, most of the townsfolk had arrived. They fell to sympathizing with my friend for his wife and for himself. Soon they prepared the dead woman's body, according to their custom.

After setting her on a bier,[20] they carried her and her husband outside the city. They walked to a mountainside at the end of the island, near the sea.

Here they lifted up a great rock. The mouth of a stone pit or well was revealed. This led down into a vast underground cave that ran beneath the mountain.

Into this pit they threw the corpse. Then, tying a rope under the husband's armpits, they lowered him down into the cavern. They gave him a big pitcher of fresh water and seven biscuits as food.

When he reached the bottom, he untied himself from the rope and they drew it up. Blocking the mouth of the pit with

---

[18]Like Christians, Moslems believe a day will come when God will raise all souls from the grave. The souls will then go to heaven or to hell for all eternity.

[19]This is not a typical Moslem custom.

[20]A bier is a stand for supporting or carrying a corpse or coffin.

the great stone, they returned to the city. Thus they left my friend in the cave with his dead wife.

When I saw this, I said to myself, "By Allah, this is a terrible way to die!"

Troubled, I sought out the King. I said to him, "O my lord, why do you bury the living with the dead?"

He said, "It has been the custom of our ancestors and our kings of old from ancient times. If the husband dies first, we bury his wife with him. It is the same with the wife. This way, they will not be separated, alive or dead."

I asked, "O King of the age, if the wife of a foreigner like myself should die in your country, would you deal with the husband in the same way?"

He answered, "Certainly. We would treat him in the manner that you saw just now."

When I heard this, my gallbladder was ready to burst. I felt violent dismay and concern for myself. My mind became dazed. It was as though I were in a horrid dungeon. I began to hate their society. I went about in fear that my wife might die before me and they would then bury me alive with her.

However, after awhile, I comforted myself. I thought, "Perhaps I shall die before her or shall have returned to my own land before she dies. No one knows who shall go first and who shall go last."

Then I applied myself to **diverting** my mind from these thoughts with various tasks.

But it was not long before my wife sickened and complained and took to her bed. After a few days, she died and passed into the hands of Allah.

The King and rest of the folk came, as was their custom, to comfort me and her family. They offered their sympathy not only for her loss but for me.

Then the women washed my wife's body and dressed her in her richest clothing and gold necklaces and jewels. Placing her on the bier, they carried her to the mountain. There they lifted the cover of the pit and cast her in.

After this all my friends and my wife's kin came round me. They bid me farewell and comforted me about my own death.

But I cried out, "Almighty Allah never made it lawful to bury the living with the dead! I am a stranger, not one of your kind. I cannot stand your custom. Had I known about it, I would never have wedded one of you!"

They paid no attention to my words. Instead, they grabbed me, bound me by force, and lowered me down into the cave. A large jug of sweet water and seven cakes of bread followed, as was customary.

When I reached the bottom, they called out to me to untie myself from the cords. But I refused to do so. So they threw the ropes down on top of me. Then, closing the mouth of the pit with the stones, they went their way.

I looked about me. I found myself in a vast cave full of dead bodies. These corpses gave off a horrid, disgusting smell. And the air was heavy with the groans of the dying.

At once, I began to blame myself for what I had done. I said to myself, "By Allah, I deserve all that has happened to me and all that shall happen to me!

"What curse was upon me that I should have taken a wife in this city? There is no Majesty and there is no Might except in Allah, the Glorious, the Great!

"As often as I say I have escaped from one **calamity**, I fall into a worse. By Allah, this is a terrible death to die! I wish to heaven that I had died a decent death and been washed and wrapped in a shroud[21] like a man and a Moslem.

"I wish that I had been drowned at sea or died in the mountains! It would have been better than this miserable death!"

---

[21]A shroud is a cloth that a corpse is wrapped in.

And I blamed myself again for my own folly and greed in that black hole, where I could not tell night from day. Nor did I cease to curse the Foul Fiend and to bless the Almighty Friend.[22]

Then I threw myself down on the bones of the dead and lay there, begging Allah's help. In the violence of my despair, I even prayed for death, which did not come to me.

Alas, the fire of hunger burned my stomach. Thirst set my throat aflame. So I sat up and felt around for the bread. I ate a bite of it, then swallowed a mouthful of water.

After this—the worst night I ever spent—I arose and explored the cave. I found that it extended a long way with many little caves along the sides. Its floor was covered with dead bodies and rotten bones that had lain there since olden times.

I finally made myself a place in a little side cave, far from the corpses lately thrown down. There I slept.

I lived in this manner till my food was ready to give out. Yet I only ate once every day or every other day. Nor did I drink more than an occasional sip. I was afraid that my supplies would run out before I died.

I said to myself, "Eat little and drink little. Perhaps the Lord will save you yet!"

One day I was sitting, pondering my situation and thinking what I should do when my bread and water ran out. Then behold! The stone that covered the opening was suddenly rolled away, and the light streamed down upon me.

I thought, "I wonder what is the matter. Maybe they have brought another corpse."

Then I spied folk standing about the mouth of the pit. In a short while they lowered down a dead man and a live woman, weeping and crying. With her was a larger supply of bread and water than usual.

---

[22]Moslems also believe in the Devil. (The Almighty Friend is, of course, Allah.)

I watched her and saw she was a beautiful woman. But she did not see me.

The opening was closed up and the mourners went away.

Then I took the leg bone of a dead man. Going up to the woman, I struck her on top of the head. She gave one cry and fell down unconscious.

I struck her a second and a third time till she was dead. Then I grabbed her bread and water. I also found on her rich garments and a great number of necklaces, jewels, and gold trinkets. It was their custom to bury women in all their finery.

I carried the food to my sleeping place and ate and drank little of it. I consumed just enough to keep me alive. Again I feared that the food should quickly run out and I would die of hunger and thirst. Yet I never completely lost hope in Almighty Allah.

I lived like this for a long time, killing all the live folk they lowered into the cave and taking their food and drink.

Finally one day, as I slept, I was awakened by something scratching and digging among the bodies in a corner of the cave. I said to myself, "What is that?" I feared it might be wolves or hyenas.

So I sprang up. Seizing the leg bone, I made for the noise. As soon as the thing noticed me, it fled deep into the cave. And lo! It was a wild beast.

I followed it to the back end. Suddenly I saw far off a point of light not bigger than a star, now appearing and then disappearing. So I headed for that.

As I drew near, the light grew larger and brighter. Finally I was certain that it was a **crevice** in the rock, leading to the open country.

I said to myself, "There must be some reason for this opening. It may be the mouth of a second pit, such as that where they lowered me. Or else it is a natural crevice in the stone."

Nearing the light, I found that it came from a crack at

the back of the mountain. The wild beasts had enlarged it by digging so that they could enter and devour the dead.

When I saw this, my spirits rose. Hope came back to me. I again became confident I would live after having died a kind of death.

So I went on, as in a dream. Scrambling through the crack, I found myself on the slope of a high mountain overlooking the salt sea. This mountain cut off all paths to the island so that none could reach that part of the beach from the city.

I praised my Lord and thanked Him, rejoicing greatly and delighting in the prospect of being saved. Then I returned through the crack to the cave and brought out all the food and water I had saved up. I also put on some of the dead folk's clothes over my own.

After this I gathered all the pearl necklaces, jewels, and trinkets of gold and silver set with precious stones. I collected these and all the other gems I could find upon the corpses.

I packed this jewelry into bundles made of the shrouds of the dead. Then I carried the treasure out to the back of the mountain facing the seashore.

There I camped. I intended to wait there till it should please Almighty Allah to send me relief by means of some passing ship.

I visited the cave daily. As often as I found folk buried alive there, I killed them all, whether they were men or women. Then I took their food and valuables to my camp on the seashore.

Thus I waited a long while. At last one day I caught sight of a ship passing through the clashing sea, swollen with dashing waves.

So I took a piece of a white shroud I had with me. Tying it to a stick, I ran along the seashore making signals with it and calling to the people in the ship.

They finally spied me and heard my shouts. At once they sent a boat to fetch me.

When it drew near, the crew called out to me. They asked, "Who are you? How have you come to be on this mountain? Never before in all our born days have we seen anyone here."

I answered, "I am a gentleman and a merchant who was shipwrecked. I saved myself (and some of my goods) by grabbing one of the ship planks.

"I was blessed by the Almighty and the decrees of Destiny and my own strength and skill. I landed in this place with my gear after a great struggle. Here I waited for some passing ship to rescue me."

Upon hearing that, they took me in their boat, along with my bundles of valuables from the cave. Then they rowed me back to the ship.

The captain greeted me and asked, "How did you end up, O sir, at that place on that mountain, behind which lies a great city? All my life I have sailed these seas and passed to and fro near these peaks. Yet I have never seen any living thing here except wild beasts and birds."

I repeated to him the story I had told the sailors. But I did not tell him anything about what had happened to me in the city or the cave for fear that there might be islanders on the ship.

Then I took out some of the best pearls I had with me. I offered them to the captain, saying, "O my lord, you have been the means of rescuing me from this mountain. I have no money. But take this to **requite** you for your kindness and good services."

However, he refused to accept my gift. He said, "When we find a shipwrecked man, we rescue him and give him meat and drink. If he is naked, we clothe him. We take nothing from him.

"Indeed, when we reach a safe port, we set him ashore with a present of our own money. We only ask him kindly to pray for us to Allah the Most High."

So I prayed that he live a long life. And I rejoiced in my

escape, trusting to be delivered from my distress. I hoped someday to forget my past misfortunes. For every time I thought about being lowered into the cave with my dead wife, I shuddered in horror.

Then we resumed our voyage. We sailed from island to island and sea to sea. Finally we arrived at the Island of the Bell. On that island stands a city that takes a man two days to cross.

From there we sailed six days until we reached the Island Kala, close to the land of Hind. This place is governed by a mighty and powerful king. It produces excellent camphor and plenty of Indian rattan.[23] There is also a lead mine here.

At last, by the decree of Allah, we arrived safely at Al Basrah. I stayed there a few days, then went on to Baghdad. Seeking out my neighborhood, I entered my house with lively pleasure. There I reunited with my family and friends. They rejoiced in my happy return and celebrated my safety.

I stored in my warehouses all the goods I had brought with me. I also gave alms and gifts to Fakirs[24] and beggars and clothed widows and orphans. Then I gave myself up to pleasure and enjoyment, returning to my old merry way of life.

Such, then, are the marvelous adventures of my fourth voyage.

[23]Camphor is a substance used in mothballs, medicine, etc. It comes from the camphor tree. Rattan is a plant used to make wickerwork.
[24]Fakirs are religious beggars who are viewed as holy men.

The date "The Voyages of Sindbad the Sailor" was written or first published is unknown. *The Arabian Nights* first appeared in a European translation in the early 1700s.

INSIGHTS INTO
THE ARABIAN NIGHTS

One of the mysteries of *The Arabian Nights* is their origin. No one knows who wrote them or when they were first dreamed up.

Some tales from the collection were first known to exist in the eighth century. However, they were not written down until the fifteenth century.

For generations, the stories were simply passed down by word of mouth. But while common folk may have loved the tales, literary circles scorned them. They felt the tales were vulgar. To them, fiction was not important enough to record.

The common folk's love for *The Arabian Nights* has not dimmed over the years. And now scholars have added their praise. The book has been called one of the most significant gifts to world literature.

Despite its name, scholars are not sure where *The Arabian Nights* came from. Israel, North Africa, Persia, and India have all been suggested as sources.

Still others say the stories are really Greek love novels. And there are those who claim the tales are soap operas for the common folk from Cairo, Egypt.

The tales of *The Arabian Nights* are united by a suspenseful framework. This framework involves a king who is betrayed by his wife. He angrily kills her and vows never to *keep* a wife again. Instead, he marries a new woman each day and takes her to bed. In the morning the bride is killed.

continued

Shahrazad, a brave young lady, determines to stop these murders. She marries the king. Then, to keep him from slaying her, she begins telling stories. The king is so fascinated that each day he spares her life.

The young wife spins out her stories for a thousand and one nights. (By that time, she has won the love of the king.) That is why *The Arabian Nights* are also called *The Thousand and One Nights*.

The Western world first became aware of *The Arabian Nights* through a translation by Antoine Galland. This Frenchman's work appeared in the early eighteenth century.

Two hundred years later another Frenchman, J.C. Mardrus, translated the tales. He claimed his version followed the original word for word.

But critics said Mardrus had been far too free with his pen. They called his work obscene. The English translator Richard Burton feared similar problems. So he carefully kept his translation under wraps.

Those who still prefer Galland's "clean" version should be aware of how freely he reworked the tales. In fact, Galland seems to have tacked some European folk tales onto his *Arabian Nights*. Among these suspect stories are the tales of Aladdin and his lamp and Ali Baba and the forty thieves.

Other stories from *The Arabian Nights*:
"The Angel of Death with the Proud King and the Devout Man"
"The Ebony Horse"
"The Fisherman and the Jinni"
"Khalifah the Fisherman of Baghdad"
"The Porter and the Three Ladies of Baghdad"
"The Tale of Kamar Al-Zaman"

THE BET

ANTON CHEKHOV

VOCABULARY PREVIEW

Below is a list of words that appear in the story. Read the list and get to know the words before you start the story.

assorted—various; different
audacious—bold and fearless
compressed—pressed together firmly and tightly
emaciated—bony; very skinny
exhaustive—complete; thorough
intact—whole and undamaged
latter—second of two things mentioned
obsolete—outdated
pinnacle—height; peak
posterity—future generations
rapture—great delight; bliss
renunciation—sacrifice or rejection
scholarly—showing great learning
scrutinize—carefully examine; study
stringently—rightly; strictly
unkempt—sloppy or untidy
vacuous—empty; bare
verified—proven or confirmed
violate—break (a rule or law)
warily—cautiously

The
BET

Anton Chekhov

Would you willingly lock yourself in one room for fifteen years? A young lawyer agrees to take such a challenge. If he lasts fifteen years, a rich banker will pay him two million.
A clear-cut bet, it seems. But in the end, you may wonder what is really at stake and who actually wins.

*I*t was a dark autumn night. The old banker was pacing from one corner of his study to the other. He was recalling a party he had given in the autumn fifteen years ago.

There were many witty people at this party and much exciting conversation. Among other topics, they had discussed capital punishment.[1]

Many scholars and journalists were attending the party. For the most part, the guests did not like capital punishment. They found it an **obsolete** custom. They said it was immoral and unsuited for

---

[1]Capital punishment is a sentence of death for a crime.

a Christian state. Some thought it should be replaced worldwide by a sentence of life in prison.

"I don't agree with you," said the host. "Of course I have never experienced capital punishment or life in prison. But if one may judge on theory, then capital punishment seems more moral and kind to me than spending your whole life in prison.

"Execution kills instantly. Life in prison kills by inches. Who is the kinder executioner: one who kills you instantly or one who saps your life steadily for years?"

"They're both equally immoral," declared one guest. "Their goal is the same—to take away life. The state is not God. It has no right to take away what it cannot give back."

Among the guests was a lawyer, a young man of about twenty-five. On being asked his opinion, he said, "Capital punishment and life in prison are equally immoral. But if I were given a choice between them, I would choose the **latter**. It's better to live in some way than not to live at all."

A lively discussion began. The banker, who was younger and higher strung then, suddenly lost his temper. He slammed his fist on the table.

Turning to the young lawyer, he cried out, "It's a lie. I bet you two million you wouldn't last in a cell for even five years."

"If you really mean it," replied the lawyer, "then I bet I could stay not just five years but fifteen."

"Fifteen! Done!" cried the banker. "Gentlemen, I wager two million."

"Agreed. You wager two million, I my freedom," said the lawyer.

So this crazy, absurd bet came to be. The banker, who had more millions than he could count at that time, was spoiled and acted on whims. Now he was beside himself with **rapture**.

During supper he said to the lawyer jokingly, "Come to your senses, young man, before it's too late. Two million doesn't mean a thing to me. But you stand to lose three or four of the best years of your life. I say three or four because you'll never last any longer.

"Don't forget, you poor fellow," the banker continued, "that willingly going to prison is much harder than being forced to go. Knowing you can free yourself at any time will poison your whole life in the cell. I feel sorry for you."

And now the banker, pacing from corner to corner, recalled all this. He asked himself, "Why did I make this bet? What's the good of it? The lawyer forfeits fifteen years of his life, and I throw away two million. Will it convince people that capital punishment is worse or better than life in prison?

"No, no! It's all nonsense. On my part, it was simply the whim of a well-fed man. On the lawyer's part, it was pure greed for gold."

He then recalled what occurred after that party long ago. It was decided the lawyer would be locked in a garden wing of the banker's house. He would be **stringently** guarded.

It was also agreed that he would not be allowed to step out the door. Nor would he be given the right to see people, hear human voices, or receive letters and newspapers.

He was permitted to have a musical instrument, read books, write letters, drink wine, and smoke tobacco. He could communicate, but only in silence, through a small window built for this purpose. Anything necessary—books, music, wine—would be sent to him when he placed a note through the window.

Every minor detail which would make his confinement totally solitary was listed in the agreement. It forced the lawyer to remain exactly fifteen years from midnight on November 14, 1870, to midnight on November 14, 1885. Any attempt to **violate** the rules—even if he escaped only two minutes before the time—freed the banker from having to pay the two million.

During the first year in his prison, the lawyer seemed to

suffer terribly. Judging by his brief notes, he seemed very lonely and bored.

From his room day and night could be heard the sound of the piano. He refused wine and tobacco. "Wine," he wrote, "arouses desires, and desires are the main enemies of a prisoner. Besides, drinking good wine by yourself is the **pinnacle** of boredom."

He went on to write that tobacco polluted the air in his room.

In the first year, he was sent humorous or light books. Usually they were novels with a complicated love story, tales of crime or fantasy, or comedies.

During the second year, the piano was silent. The lawyer only asked for classics.

In the fifth year, music could be heard again. The prisoner requested wine, too. Those who watched him said that he only ate, drank, and reclined on his bed the whole year.

Apart from that, he yawned often and talked angrily to himself. He did not read books.

Sometimes at night he sat down to write. He would write for a long time and then tear everything up in the morning. On more than one occasion, he was heard weeping.

In the latter half of the sixth year, the prisoner began to study languages, philosophy, and history with zeal. He tackled these subjects so eagerly that the banker could scarcely get enough books for him. In four years' time about six hundred volumes were sent to him.

During this fit of passion the banker received this letter from the prisoner.

"My dear jailor, I write these lines in six languages. Show them to experts. Let them **scrutinize** them.

"If they do not find a single mistake, I beg you order a gun fired off in the garden. By the noise, I shall know my labor has not been in vain.

"The geniuses of all ages and nations speak in various languages. But in all of them burns the same flame.

"Oh, if you only realized my heavenly happiness now that I can understand them!"

The prisoner's wish was complied with. Two shots were fired in the garden under the banker's order.

After the tenth year, the lawyer sat motionless before his table. There he remained, reading only the New Testament.

The banker found it odd that he should spend a year reading just one book. After all, this book was easy to understand and not thick at all. The lawyer had mastered six hundred **scholarly** works in just four years.

When the lawyer finished the New Testament, he began studying the history of religions and theology.[2]

During the last two years, the prisoner read an amazing amount. And it was extremely **assorted** material.

First, he would devote himself to the study of the natural sciences. Then he would move on to Byron[3] and Shakespeare.

He used to send notes asking for books. He would request at the same time a text on chemistry and one on medicine, a novel, and works on philosophy or theology. He waded through the books as though he were swimming in a sea among pieces of wreckage. In his desire to save his life, he was eagerly grasping one piece after another.

II

The banker recalled all this and thought, "Tomorrow at midnight he will be freed. Under our agreement, I shall have to hand over two million. But if I pay, I'm finished. I'll be ruined forever—"

Fifteen years before, he had more millions than he knew what to do with. But now he was afraid to ask himself which he had more of, money or debts.

[2]Theology is the study of religious beliefs.

[3]George Gordon, Lord Byron (1788-1824) was an English poet.

He thought over his life: gambling on the stock market, risky investments, and life-long recklessness. For all those reasons, his business had gradually decayed. The once **audacious**, confident, proud man was gone. He had become a humble banker, trembling at every rise and fall in the market.

"That damned bet," muttered the old man, clutching his head in agony. "Why didn't the man die? But he's only forty years old. He will take away my last penny. Then he'll marry, enjoy life, gamble on the market.

"Meanwhile, I'll be looking on like an envious beggar. Day after day, he'll say the same words to me: 'I owe you the happiness of my life. Let me help you.'

"No, it's too much! There's only one escape from bankruptcy and shame. The man must die."

The clock had just chimed three. The banker listened. Everyone in the house was asleep. Only the frozen trees screeching outside the windows could be heard.

Trying to be perfectly silent, he took from the safe the key to the door which had been closed for fifteen years. Then he put on his overcoat and stole out of the house.

The garden was dark and cold. It was raining. A damp, sharp wind roared in the garden and gave the trees no rest. The banker strained to peer through the darkness, but he could not see the ground, the white statues, the garden wing, or the trees.

Nearing the garden wing, he called out twice to the watchman. There was no reply. Apparently the watchman had taken shelter from the rain. He was probably sleeping in the greenhouse.

"If I have the courage to carry out my plan," thought the old man, "they'll suspect the watchman first."

In the darkness he felt for the steps and door. When he found them, he entered the hall of the garden wing. He poked his way into a narrow passage and lit a match. Not a soul was there. Someone's bed—without a cover—and an iron stove loomed dark in the corner.

The seals on the door of the prisoner's room were still **intact** and unbroken.

The match went out. The old man, nervously shaking, peered into the little window.

In the prisoner's room a candle burned dimly. The prisoner himself sat by the table. Only his back, hair, and hands were visible. Open books were scattered on the table, chairs, and carpet.

Five minutes passed. In all that time the prisoner never once stirred. After fifteen years in prison, he had learned how to sit motionless.

The banker rapped on the window with his finger. But the prisoner did not respond with any movement. Then the banker **warily** tore the seals from the door and put the key into the lock.

The rusty lock groaned and the door creaked. The banker expected a cry of surprise and footsteps to follow.

He waited three minutes. Still it was as quiet inside as before. He decided to enter.

In front of the table sat a man not like any normal human being. He was a skeleton, with tight skin, long curly hair like a woman's, and an **unkempt** beard.

His complexion was yellow and brownish. The cheeks were sunken, the back long and lean. The hand upon which he rested his hairy head was so skinny that it was painful to look at it. His hair was already greying. No one who saw his ancient, **emaciated** face would have believed he was only forty.

On the table lay a piece of paper. Something was written on it in small letters.

"Poor devil," thought the banker. "He's asleep and probably seeing millions in his dreams. I have only to throw this half-dead thing down and smother him with the pillow. The most **exhaustive** examination would not find a trace of murder.

"But, first, let me see what he has written here."

The banker took the sheet from the table and read the letter.

"Tomorrow at midnight, I will again gain my freedom and the right to join society. But before I leave this room and step into the sun, I think I should say a few words to you.

"Upon my clear conscience and before God, I swear that I scorn freedom and health. I scorn life. I scorn these things and all that your books call blessings of earthly existence.

"For fifteen years I have diligently studied this earthly life. True, I could not observe the earth or its people. But, through your books, I drank wine and sang songs. I hunted deer and wild boars in the forests. I loved women.

"And beautiful women, like the airiest of clouds, visited me at night. I met these women through the magic words of your gifted poets. The women would come and whisper to me wonderful tales which made my head swim.

"Through your books, I climbed to the peaks of Elburz and Mont Blanc.[4] There I saw how the sun rose in the morning. Then I saw it flood the evening sky, the sea, and mountains with a purple gold. I saw above me lightning bolts shining as they split the clouds.

"I saw green woods, fields, rivers, lakes, and cities. I heard sirens singing, and Pan playing his pipes.[5] I touched the wings of beautiful devils who flew to me to speak of God.

"Through your books, I threw myself into bottomless pits. I performed miracles and burned cities to the ground.

---

[4]The Elburz Mountains stand in Iran. Mont Blanc is the highest mountain in the Alps. It is located at the border between Italy, France, and Switzerland.

[5]Sirens are half-woman, half-bird creatures from ancient Greek myths. They lured sailors into a death trap by singing a lovely song. Pan was the Greek god of the forest. He was known for his musical ability with the pipes.

I preached new religions and conquered entire nations.

"Your books made me wise. All that tireless human knowledge, gathered through the centuries, is **compressed** into my skull. I know that I am cleverer than all of you.

"And I scorn your books, scorn all blessings and wisdom of this world. Everything is as **vacuous**, weak, and unreal as a mirage. You may be proud, wise, and beautiful. Yet death will wipe you from the face of the earth, like mice in their holes.

"Your **posterity**, your history, and the fame of your geniuses will be melted down like frozen scum. It will all burn down. Your earth will burn down, too.

"You are insane and have gone the wrong way. You accept lies as truth and take ugliness for beauty. You would be astounded if apple and orange trees should suddenly bear frogs and lizards instead of fruit. If roses should all at once smell like sweating horses, you would be amazed.

"But I am equally amazed at you. You have traded heaven for earth. I do not want to understand you.

"I will show you my contempt for your way of life. I will give up my right to the two million which I once dreamed would be heaven. I will reject it by leaving this room five minutes before the agreed time. By that act, I will have broken the agreement."

When he had finished reading, the banker put the paper back on the table. He kissed the head of the strange man and began to weep. He left the wing.

Never before—not even when he lost a fortune on the stock market—had he scorned himself so much. Going back to his room, he lay down on his bed. But his tears kept him awake for a long time.

Next morning the poor watchman came running to the banker. He reported that they had seen the man who lived in the wing climb out the window into the garden. He had gone to the gate and disappeared.

The banker at once went with his servants and **verified**

that the prisoner had escaped. To stop any rumors, he took the paper with the **renunciation** from the table. Returning to the house, he locked it in his safe.

"The Bet" was first published in 1888.

INSIGHTS INTO
ANTON CHEKHOV

(1860-1904)

Chekhov was born in Taganrog, Russia.

Chekhov was first moved to write just to make money.

After Chekhov's father went bankrupt, the family was in serious difficulty. So to help support them, Chekhov began writing jokes and short sketches. He was paid a penny a line.

"Do you know how I write my little tales?" Chekhov once asked a writer friend. "Well, here you are."

Chekhov looked around the table and picked up the first thing to catch his eye. It was an ashtray.

"Tomorrow, if you wish, there will be a story."

The vow produced Chekhov's story "The Ashtray."

Chekhov described his play *The Sea Gull* in terms of a recipe.

It's "a comedy, three female parts, six male, four acts, landscape (view of a lake), lots of talk about literature, little action, and five tons of love."

The recipe seemed a disaster at first. Critics who went to opening night called the play "entirely absurd," "dull," and "false." Even a friend of Chekhov's who wrote a review said it was not "the Seagull, but simply a wild fowl."

The play reopened two years later. This time it was a huge success. *The Sea Gull* went on to become a classic of modern theater.

While traveling on ship once, Chekhov had a terrible fright. A typhoon crossed the path of the ship. The heavy wind and waves nearly turned the vessel on its side.

The captain advised Chekhov to keep a gun handy. That

continued

way, if the ship sank, Chekhov could spare himself a long death. Fortunately, the ship rode out the storm.

On top of this, Chekhov saw the burial at sea of two passengers. It frightened him to watch the bodies tumble into the water. He imagined them sinking to the deep sea floor.

Chekhov captured the horror of his trip in the short story "Gusev." He even completed the tale during the course of the voyage!

In the early stages of his career, Chekhov did not claim his work as his own. Instead, he used pen names like "The Brother of my Brother" and "Rover." Another title the humble physician chose to use was "Doctor without Patients."

Chekhov's real name first appeared on his work with the publication of *Motley Stories* in 1886. It was lucky that Chekhov chose that moment to reveal his identity. *Motley Stories* was his first claim to fame.

Chekhov was a doctor. But he certainly did not pursue the career for money. In a year's time alone, he probably treated a thousand poor people for free.

Sadly, Chekhov's knowledge was wasted on himself. He ignored a nagging cough and other health problems for years. Only after a serious collapse did he let another doctor examine him.

The diagnosis: tuberculosis. The disease eventually killed him.

Other works by Chekhov:
   "Anna on the Neck," short story
   "The Darling," short story
   "Gooseberries," short story
   "The Lady with the Dog," short story
   The Cherry Orchard, play
   The Three Sisters, play
   Uncle Vanya, play

THE NIGHTINGALE

HANS CHRISTIAN ANDERSEN

VOCABULARY PREVIEW

Below is a list of words that appear in the story. Read the list and get to know the words before you start the story.

august—lordly and grand

coquettishness—playfulness; behavior that is flirtatious

courtier—one who serves or is often present in a monarch's court

daunting—dismaying or frightening

denounced—criticized or blamed

dispersed—scattered

domain—territory or sphere one controls

embedded—firmly stuck in an object

enthralled—fascinated; spellbound

exquisite—rare and delicately beautiful

imperial—of or concerning an empire or ruler of an empire

inscription—words and other markings printed or carved on a surface

lulled—soothed or caused to rest

milled—moved around in a confused manner

plebeian—lowborn; common

predetermined—settled and fixed in advance

recompensed—repaid or rewarded

regale—entertain in rich fashion

renowned—famous

sanctity—holiness or sacredness

The Nightingale

In the Emperor's garden behind his glorious palace lies the loveliest treasure in China: a nightingale. Her song is enough to enchant both poor and rich.

Yet a gift from the Emperor of Japan dulls the Chinese Emperor's fondness for his nightingale. Only when he comes face to face with Death does the Chinese Emperor realize his songbird's true beauty.

In China, as you know, the Emperor is Chinese, and all the people around him are also Chinese.

It is a great many years since all this happened. But that's a good reason for hearing the story, before it's forgotten.

The Emperor's palace was the most wonderful one in the world. It was made entirely of fine porcelain. This made it costly but fragile. You had to be very careful whenever you touched it.

Hans Christian Andersen

In the garden the most marvelous flowers were to be seen. The loveliest of them all were hung with little silver bells. These bells continually tinkled so that nobody could pass by without stopping to look.

Every part of the Emperor's garden was most cleverly thought out. And it was so big that even the gardener did not know how far it went.

If you kept on walking, you came at last to a wondrous forest with lofty trees and deep lakes. The forest went down to the edge of a deep, blue sea. This sea was deep enough so that large ships could sail close in under the tree branches.

Among those trees lived a nightingale. Her song was so gorgeous that even the poor fisherman—who had many other things to do—would stop and listen as he drew in his nets at night.

"How beautiful!" he said. But since he had to attend to his work, he quickly forgot the bird.

But the next night, when the fisherman would hear the nightingale sing again, he would repeat, "How beautiful!"

Travelers from all over the world came to the Emperor's capital. They admired everything in the city, particularly the palace and garden. But when they heard the nightingale, all of them said, "That's the most **exquisite** thing of all."

They would talk about their visit when they returned to their country. Learned men wrote many books about the city, the palace, and the garden.

But no one forgot about the nightingale. In fact, the travelers praised her above everything else. Those who were poets wrote beautiful verses about the nightingale in the forest by the deep, blue sea.

These books went all over the world. Eventually some of them reached the Emperor. Sitting in his golden chair, he read and read. Now and again he nodded his head, delighted to see such glowing descriptions of the city, palace, and garden.

"But the nightingale is the most exquisite thing of all," he read.

"What does this mean!" said the Emperor. "The nightingale? I've never heard of it. Can there be such a bird in my **domain** and in my very own garden without my knowing it? Imagine having to find this out from books!"

Then he called his top aide, a gentleman-in-waiting.[1] This aide was so vain that if a person lower in rank dared to speak to him or ask him questions, he answered nothing but "Pah!" And of course that means nothing at all.

"I have learned that we have a very remarkable bird here called a nightingale," said the Emperor. "They say she is the most exquisite thing in all my great domain. Why have I never been told anything about this bird?"

"I have never heard of her before," said the aide. "She has never been presented at court."

"I order her to come and sing for me this evening," said the Emperor. "I cannot believe this! The whole world knows that I possess this treasure while I know nothing about it!"

"I have never heard of her before," repeated the aide. "Yet I will look for her and find her, too."

But where was the nightingale to be found? The aide ran up and down every staircase in the palace. He checked in all the rooms and each corridor. But no one he met had ever heard of the nightingale.

So the aide ran back to the Emperor. He reported that the nightingale had to be a myth invented by the book writers. "Your **Imperial** Majesty must not believe all that is written! Books are just inventions, even though they can't really be called black magic."

"But the book in which I have read this was sent to me by the **august** Emperor of Japan," said the Emperor. "Therefore it must be true. I insist upon hearing the nightingale this very evening. I offer her my most gracious welcome. And if she does not appear, I will have the entire court beaten after supper."

---

[1] A gentleman-in-waiting is a man appointed to attend or serve a ruler.

"Tsing-pe!" said the aide. Away he started again. Upstairs and downstairs, through rooms and corridors he ran. Half the court went with him, for none of them were very eager to be beaten after supper. They asked everywhere about this remarkable nightingale which was known the world over—except to the court.

At last they found a poor little maid in the kitchen. She said, "Oh my, the nightingale? I know her well. Indeed she can sing! Every evening I am allowed to take tablescraps to my poor sick mother who lives down by the shore.

"On my way home, when I stop to rest in the forest, I hear the nightingale. Listening to her brings tears into my eyes. I feel as if my mother were kissing me."

"Little kitchen maid," said the aide, "Will you lead us to the nightingale? If you do, I will get you a permanent place in the palace kitchen. I will even get permission for you to see the Emperor dine—She has been ordered to appear at court this evening."

So they went to the forest where the nightingale usually sang. Half the court followed as well.

As they hurried along, a cow began to moo.

"Oh!" cooed the **courtiers**. "That's her! What marvelous volume for such a tiny creature! I'm sure I've heard her song before."

"No, that's a cow mooing," said the little kitchen maid. "We are still a long way from the place."

Then the courtiers heard some frogs in the pond begin to croak.

"Beautiful!" sighed the Chinese court chaplain. "The nightingale sounds like the tinkling of little church bells."

"No, that's the frogs," said the little kitchen maid. "But I think we shall soon hear her."

Then the nightingale began to sing.

"Listen, listen! It's her," cried the little girl. "There she sits." She pointed to a little gray bird up in the branches.

"Is it possible?" exclaimed the aide. "I should never have

thought she was like that. How **plebeian** she looks! But perhaps she lost her color when she saw herself among so many grand people!"

"Little nightingale!" called out the kitchen maid. "Our Gracious Emperor wishes you to sing for him."

"With the greatest of pleasure," replied the nightingale. She sang away in a voice that was sheer delight.

"It sounds like glass bells," judged the aide. "And look at her little throat, it throbs so! It's incredible that we've never heard her before. I'm confident that bird will be a great success at court."

"Shall I sing once more before the Emperor?" asked the nightingale. She thought that the Emperor was present.

"My dear little nightingale," said the aide, "I have great pleasure in ordering you to appear at a court ball this evening. There you will **regale** His Imperial Majesty with your bewitching song."

"My song sounds best in the forest," replied the nightingale. However, she went with them willingly when she heard it was the Emperor's wish.

Everything in the palace had been beautifully polished for that event. The walls and floors, which were all made of china, gleamed in the light of thousands of gold lamps.

Gorgeous flowers with jingling bells were placed in the corridors. There was so much racing back and forth that a great draft was created. This set all the little bells jingling and jangling and drowned out all other noise.

In the middle of the enormous reception hall near the Emperor's throne, a golden perch had been set for the nightingale. The entire court was gathered there. Even the little kitchen maid was present. Since she had been promoted to cook, she was allowed to stand behind the door.

They were all dressed in their best clothes. Everyone stared at the little gray bird to whom the Emperor gave a charming nod.

And the nightingale sang beautifully. So beautifully, in

fact, that tears came into the Emperor's eyes and rolled down his cheeks. And then the nightingale sang still more beautifully. Its song melted everyone's heart.

The Emperor was so **enthralled** that he wanted the little bird to wear his golden slipper round her neck. But the nightingale declined the gift with thanks. She already felt generously rewarded.

She said, "I have seen tears in the Emperor's eyes. That is the most valuable gift for me! An Emperor's tears hold a marvelous power. Heaven knows I have been more than **recompensed**." And she trilled again her sweet, blessed song.

"That was the most delightful **coquettishness** I've ever heard," said the ladies present. They tried filling their mouths with water to produce a gurgling sound whenever they spoke. They imagined that by doing this they sounded like nightingales themselves.

Even the butlers and the maids revealed that they were quite pleased. And that is saying a great deal, for servants are always the most difficult to satisfy.

It was fact; the nightingale was a tremendous success.

After that, the nightingale was ordered to stay at court. She was presented with her own cage. Permission was granted for her to go for a walk twice a day and once at night. Twelve servants were to accompany her. Each one held on tightly to a ribbon fastened to the bird's leg. There was not much delight at all in that kind of outing.

The entire town talked about the amazing bird. When two people met, one of them could hardly bid the other "Night—" before the other responded "Gale!" And then they sighed, expressing their deep understanding of one another.

The public passion was so great that eleven butchers' children were named after the nightingale. However, not even one of them could sing a note in tune.

One day a large parcel arrived for the Emperor. On the outside was written "Nightingale."

"It has to be another book about our **renowned** bird," said the Emperor.

But it wasn't a book. Inside the box was a small work of art: an artificial nightingale. It was an exact copy of the living bird but **embedded** with diamonds, rubies, and sapphires all over.

When the bird was wound up, it could sing one of the tunes the real nightingale sang. While it warbled, its tail flipped up and down, glittering with silver and gold.

A ribbon was tied around its neck. It bore this **inscription**: "The nightingale of the Emperor of Japan is poor compared to that of the Emperor of China."

"It's amazing!" they all exclaimed. The one who had brought the artificial bird immediately received the title of "Head Imperial Carrier of the Nightingale."

"Now we must hear them sing together," said someone. "What a duet that will be!"

So they had to sing together. But it did not sound very pleasant. The real nightingale sang in her own way while the artificial bird mechanically warbled its notes.

"We can't criticize the artificial bird," said the music master. "It keeps time perfectly and sings exactly in tune."

Then the artificial bird had to sing by itself. It was just as great a success as the real bird. Besides that, it was much prettier to look at. It sparkled like bracelets and jeweled pins.

Thirty-three times it sang the same tune over. Yet it wasn't the slightest bit tired. The courtiers would willingly have heard it from the start all over again.

However, the Emperor thought that the real nightingale should sing a little. But where was she? No one had noticed that she had flown out the open window, back to her own green forests.

"What is the meaning of this?" demanded the Emperor.

All the courtiers furiously **denounced** the nightingale. They maintained that she was a most ungrateful creature.

"Fortunately, we still have the best bird," they said. Then

they again asked that the artificial bird sing. And for the thirty-fourth time they listened to the same tune. They still did not know it by heart yet because the song was very difficult.

The music master greatly praised the artificial bird. He maintained that it was better than the real nightingale. He pointed out that not only did the artificial bird have a diamond-studded body, it also had a superior mechanical interior.

"You see, ladies and gentlemen—and Your Imperial Majesty above all—with the real nightingale, one can never be sure what it will next sing. But with the artificial bird, everything is **predetermined**. You know what to expect, and you'll always know what to expect.

"The mechanical workings of this bird can be explained. You can take it apart and show the human skill involved in making the bird. You can see how one action leads to a reaction."

"That is exactly what I think!" each courtier declared.

The music master received permission to show the bird to all the people on the next Sunday.

"They must hear it, too," said the Emperor.

The public did hear it. And they all were as dazzled as if they had taken a drop too much tea—a truly Chinese custom.

"Oh!" was heard from every mouth. And they all wagged their fingers and nodded.

But the poor fisherman who had heard the real nightingale said, "It does sound quite nice—it's almost like the real bird. But there's something missing. I don't know what."

In the meantime, the real nightingale was exiled from the kingdom.

The artificial bird had its place on a silken cushion next to the Emperor's bed. All the gifts of gold and precious gems which the bird had received were placed round it.

It had now been given the title of "High Imperial Singer

of the Bedroom.'' It was number one in rank on the left side. To the Emperor, that was the most important side because that is the side of the body where the heart is located. Even the heart of an Emperor is on the left.

The music master wrote twenty-five volumes about the artificial bird. The work was very dull and was full of the most difficult Chinese words. But everybody said they had read and understood it. Otherwise they would have been called stupid and would have been beaten.

A whole year passed in this manner. The Emperor, the court, and all the other Chinese knew by heart every low and every high of the artificial bird's song. But that was why they liked it so much. That way they were able to join in the singing. Even the boys in the street sang ''Zee, zee, zee; glu, glu, glu!'' The Emperor sang it, too.

One evening when the bird was in the midst of its song and the Emperor was lying in bed and listening, something clicked inside the bird. Then it snapped with a ''Clunk, clunk.'' The wheels churned round and the music stopped.

The Emperor leaped out of bed and summoned his physicians. But what use could they be?

Then the watchmaker was summoned. After a great deal of talk and checking, he repaired the bird as well as he was able.

But he said the bird should be wound up only very rarely. The cogs were almost worn out. And he could not put in new ones to make the music sound as perfect as before.

This was sad news, indeed! Only once a year was the artificial bird allowed to sing. Even that was almost too much of a strain. At those times the music master made a little speech, using all the most difficult words. He asserted that the song was just as good as ever. Because he said so, it seemed it was so.

Five years had gone by when a great sorrow suddenly struck the kingdom. Deep down, the people were very fond of the Emperor. Now he was ill and it was gossiped that he could not possibly live. A new Emperor had already been selected.

People **milled** about in the street and asked the gentleman-in-waiting how the Emperor was doing.

"Pah!" he said, then shook his head.

Pale and cold, the Emperor lay in his beautiful bed. The courtiers believed he was dead. They hurried off to honor the new Emperor. The butlers ran out to gossip, and the maids gave a huge tea party.

Carpets had been laid down in all the rooms and corridors to muffle the sound of footsteps. The palace was wrapped in a deep silence.

But the Emperor was not dead yet. He lay stiff and pale in his beautiful bed with the velvet curtains and heavy gold tassels. High up a window had been opened. Now the moon beamed down on him and on the artificial bird.

The poor Emperor could hardly breathe. Something seemed to be sitting on his chest, keeping him from breathing.

He opened his eyes and saw that it was Death. Death had put on the Emperor's golden crown. In one hand he held the imperial golden sword, in the other the imperial banner.

Weird faces peered out from between the folds of the velvet curtains. Some were terrifying; others were gentle and appealing. These were all the Emperor's good and bad deeds. They were watching him now that Death was pressing on his heart.

"Do you remember this? And do you remember that?" they whispered one after another. They told him so many things that the sweat flowed down his face.

"I never knew about any of these things," said the Emperor. "Music! music! Play the huge Chinese drum to drown out these voices!"

But the whispers did not cease. And Death nodded in Chinese fashion at every word that was spoken.

"Music, music!" screamed the Emperor. "Dear little

golden bird, sing, please, sing! I have heaped gold and precious gems on you. I even hung my golden slipper round your neck. Sing, I beg you, sing!"

But the bird remained silent. There was no one to wind it up, so naturally it could not sing.

With his great empty eye sockets, Death kept staring at the Emperor. The silence became deeper and more **daunting**.

Suddenly through the window floated a gorgeous song. It was the living nightingale, sitting on a branch outside. She had heard of her Emperor's illness and had come to bring him hope and comfort.

As she sang, the weird faces grew paler and paler. Meanwhile the blood flowed with new strength through the Emperor's frail body.

Death himself listened and said, "Sing, little nightingale, sing!"

"Yes, I will if you give me the glorious golden sword. Yes, if you give me the gorgeous banner. And, yes, if you give me the Emperor's crown."

Death handed over each of these treasures for a tune, and the nightingale sang on. She sang about the quiet churchyard where roses bloom. She sang about the elder flowers there that filled the air with fragrance. And she sang about the fresh green grass, sprinkled with mourners' tears.

The song touched Death with a longing for his own quiet garden. Like a cold white mist, he faded out of the window.

"Thank you, thank you!" said the Emperor. "You heavenly little bird, I remember you very well. It was you I exiled from my Empire. Yet your song has **dispersed** the evil visions from my bed and driven Death himself from my heart. How can I ever reward you?"

"You have already rewarded me," replied the nightingale. "Tears came to your eyes the first time I sang to you. I shall never forget that. Those are the jewels that delight a singer's heart.

"But go to sleep now, and wake up whole and strong again. I will sing to you."

Then she sang again. The Emperor was **lulled** into a sweet, healing sleep.

The sun was shining through the window on him when he awoke. He was well and strong. Not one of his servants had come to his room. They all believed him to be dead. But the little nightingale still sang.

"You must stay with me always," said the Emperor. "You shall only sing when you feel like it. Moreover, I will break the artificial bird into a thousand pieces."

"Don't do that," said the nightingale. "It did all that it was able to do. Keep it as you did before. I cannot nest here and live in the palace, but do let me come whenever I wish. In the evening I will sit outside and sing to you.

"My song will gladden you and make you thoughtful as well. I will sing about happy people and about those who suffer. I will sing about the good and the evil in your domain that is kept hidden from you.

"The little songbird flies far and wide, to the hut of the poor fisherman or the house of the lowly farmer. I seek out many who are a long way from you and your court.

"Your heart is more dear to me than your crown. Yet the crown has an odor of **sanctity** about it. I will come and I will sing to you. But you must promise me one thing."

"Anything!" vowed the Emperor. And there he stood in his imperial robes, holding the sword heavy with gold against his heart.

"One thing only I ask of you. Do not tell anyone that you have a little bird who tells you everything. It will be better that way."

Then the nightingale flew off.

The servants came in to check on their dead Emperor. And there he stood, greeting them all with a hearty "Good morning!"

"The Nightingale" was first published in 1843.

INSIGHTS INTO HANS CHRISTIAN ANDERSEN

(1805-1875)

Andersen was born in Odense, Denmark.

Andersen was born into extreme poverty. His mother and father had to make most of the furniture for their home. The bed was actually a wooden frame once used to hold a count's coffin.

But from that grisly beginning came a happy result. In 1805, Hans Christian Andersen was born in the bed.

When he was just six, Andersen visited the insane asylum where his grandmother worked. There he would tell stories to the patients. In turn, they "entertained" him with horrid stories of witches, ghosts, disease, and death. This experience further sparked the boy's already active imagination.

Andersen always believed he would be famous. This confidence was evident even in his youth. He left his home at the age of 14, penniless. Yet he stated, "I'm going to Copenhagen to become famous."

Two fears obsessed Andersen. One was the fear that he had left a candle burning in a room he had just left. He would go back again and again to check.

Andersen was also afraid of missing trains. He drove traveling companions crazy by insisting they get to the station hours before the train left.

Andersen looked like a stork. He was constantly teased and tormented about his long awkward body.

continued

The taunts were the basis for Andersen's fairy tale "The Ugly Duckling." The title character was really the author himself. Andersen believed that, like his duckling, he grew into a beautiful swan.

At the end of Andersen's rocky life, he still maintained, "Life itself is the most wonderful fairy tale of all."

Other works by Andersen:
"The Emperor's New Clothes," short story
"The Little Match Girl," short story
"The Princess and the Pea," short story
"The Snow Queen," short story
"Thumbelina," short story
Improvisatoren, book

GOD SEES THE TRUTH, BUT WAITS

LEO TOLSTOY

VOCABULARY PREVIEW

Below is a list of words that appear in the story. Read the list and get to know the words before you start the story.

adequate—enough; satisfactory
ambled—strolled
congregated—gathered; assembled
despondent—despairing or downcast
disconsolate—depressed and downhearted
disposed—gotten rid of
forlorn—lonesome and wretched
incessantly—continually; never stopping
interrogating—cross-examining; questioning
merriment—lightheartedness and glee
petition—make a formal, written plea; request
premature—too early
reiterated—repeated
reminisced—remembered
swooned—fainted
tribulation—great distress or trouble
unruly—rowdy
upright—honest and moral
vivacious—lively and free-spirited
wares—goods

GOD SEES THE TRUTH, BUT WAITS

Leo Tolstoy

One day Ivan Aksionov is a wealthy, carefree merchant; the next an accused murderer. The change is all the more horrifying because he's innocent and no one will believe him.

Yet the truth has a way of surfacing in the strangest manner—even if it takes twenty-six years.

*I*n the village of Vladimir there lived a young merchant named Ivan Dmitrich Aksionov. He owned two shops and a house.

Ivan was a handsome, blond, curly-haired fellow. He was **vivacious** and loved to sing. In his younger days, he had been in the habit of drinking a lot. When he drank too much, he grew **unruly**.

But marriage changed that. He had given up drinking—except now and then.

One summer Ivan set out for the Nizhny Fair. As he said goodbye to his family, his wife said, "Ivan Dmitrich, don't leave today. I had a nightmare about you."

Ivan laughed. He said, "You're just afraid that I'll lose my head when I get to the fair."

His wife replied, "I do not know why I am afraid. I just know that I had a nightmare. In my dream, I saw you return from town. When you removed your cap, I could see that your hair was entirely grey."

Ivan laughed. "That's a good sign," he said. "Just watch. I'll sell all my goods and bring back gifts from the fair."

With that he said goodbye to his family and drove off.

After he had traveled about halfway, he met a merchant whom he knew. They stopped at the same inn for the night. After having tea together, they went to bed in rooms next to each other.

Ivan rarely slept late. Wanting to set out while it was still cool, he wakened his driver before daybreak and told him to ready the horses.

Then he sought out the landlord of the inn. (This gentleman lived in a little house at the back.) After paying his bill, Ivan continued his journey.

He had gone about twenty-five miles when he decided to stop and have the horses fed. He rested for a bit in the hall of the inn. Then he **ambled** out onto the porch. Ordering some tea, he got out his guitar and started to strum it.

Suddenly a troika[1] pulled up with tiny, ringing bells. An official got out, along with two soldiers. He approached Ivan and began to question him. He asked him who he was and where he came from.

Ivan answered all the questions. Then he asked, "Will you join me for some tea?"

---

[1]A troika is a Russian vehicle pulled by three horses.

But the official went on questioning him. He asked, "Where did you stay last night? Were you alone or was another merchant with you? Did you see that merchant today? Why did you leave the inn before daybreak?"

Ivan was puzzled at being asked all these questions. But he explained all that had happened. Then he added, "Why are you questioning me as if I were a robber or a thief? I'm on personal business, and there's no reason to question me."

Summoning the soldiers, the official replied, "I am the police officer of this district. I've been **interrogating** you because of the merchant you roomed next to last night. He has been found with his throat cut. We must search your things."

They went inside the house. The soldiers and the officer opened Ivan's bags and searched them.

Suddenly the officer pulled a knife out of one bag. He exclaimed, "Who does this knife belong to?"

Seeing a blood-stained knife taken from his luggage, Ivan was terrified.

"Why is there blood on this knife?" demanded the officer.

Ivan struggled to reply, but he could scarcely utter a word. He was only able to stammer, "I—don't know—it's not mine."

Then the police officer said, "The merchant was found in bed this morning with his throat cut. You're the only one who could have done it. The house was bolted from inside. No one else was there.

"And, now, here's a blood-stained knife in your luggage. Your face and manner show you're guilty! Confess how you murdered him and how much of his money you took."

Ivan swore he had not done it. He protested that he had last seen the merchant when they had tea together. Moreover, the eight thousand rubles[2] Ivan had with him

---

[2] A ruble is a piece of Russian currency.

were all his own. As for the knife, why, it was not his.

But even as he explained, Ivan's voice shook, his face went white, and he trembled with fear. He looked just like a guilty man.

The police officer ordered the soldiers to tie Ivan and to take him to the cart. As they bound his feet and tossed him into the cart, Ivan crossed himself[3] and wept. His money and **wares** were seized. He was sent to the jail in the nearest town.

In Vladimir, the police checked into Ivan Aksionov's past. The merchants and other citizens reported that Ivan used to drink and waste his time. But they added that he was a good man now.

Then came the trial. Ivan was accused of murdering a merchant from Ryazan and stealing twenty thousand rubles from him.

His wife was **forlorn** and did not know what to think. All her children were small. In fact, one was still a nursing baby.

The wife gathered the children up and headed to the town where her husband was imprisoned.

At first she was not allowed to see him. After much begging, the officials granted permission and she was allowed to see him.

She **swooned** when she found her husband in prison clothes and in chains, jailed with thieves and criminals. She did not come to her senses for quite a while.

Then she gathered her children close and sat near her husband. She gave him news from home and asked about what he had been through.

After he told her his story, she asked, "What can we do now?"

---

[3]Crossing oneself is to make the sign of the cross. It is a gesture Catholics make in reverence for God.

"We must **petition** the Tsar[4] not to let an innocent man die."

His wife said that she had sent a petition to the Tsar but it had been turned down.

Ivan fell silent, looking **disconsolate**.

Then his wife said, "That dream about your hair turning grey meant something after all. Do you remember? You should not have left that day."

Running her fingers through his hair, she said, "Dear Vanya, tell your wife the truth. It was you who did it, wasn't it?"

"Even you suspect me!" cried Ivan. He covered his face with his hands and began to weep.

Then a soldier came to say that the family must leave. Ivan bid his family goodbye for the final time.

After they had left, Ivan recalled what had been said. He remembered that his wife also had doubted his innocence. He said to himself, "It seems that only God knows the truth. We must petition God alone. Only from Him can we expect mercy."

So Ivan did not send any more petitions. He gave up all hope and only prayed to God.

Ivan was sentenced to be whipped and sent to the mines. So he was whipped. When his wounds had healed, he was driven to Siberia[5] with other prisoners.

For twenty-six years Ivan lived in Siberia as a prisoner. His hair turned white as snow. His beard grew long, scraggly, and grey. All the **merriment** went out of his nature. He walked slowly and with a stoop. Though rarely speaking and never laughing, he often prayed.

In prison Ivan learned to make boots. By means of his trade, he earned a bit of money, with which he bought *The*

---

[4]Tsar was once the title for a male ruler of Russia.

[5]Siberia is a cold section in eastern Russia. Criminals are sometimes sent there.

Lives of the Saints.[6] He read this book when there was **adequate** light in the prison.

On Sundays in the prison church, he read lessons. He sang in the choir too, for he still had a nice voice.

The prison officials liked Ivan because he was obedient.

His fellow-prisoners looked up to him as well. They called him "Grandfather" and "The Saint." When they wanted to request the prison authorities for anything, they always made Ivan their spokesman. When arguments occurred among the prisoners, they came to him to judge and settle things.

Ivan received no news from home. He did not even know if his wife and children were still alive.

One day a fresh gang of prisoners arrived. That night the old prisoners **congregated** round the new ones. They wanted to know what towns or villages the newcomers came from and their crimes.

Ivan sat down with the rest near the newcomers. He listened with a sorrowful ear to what was said.

One of the newcomers was telling the other why he had been arrested. This convict was a tall, hearty man, about sixty years old. He wore a closely-shaved, grey beard.

"Well, friends," he said, "I only took a horse that was tied to a sleigh. They arrested me and charged me with theft. I told them I'd only taken it to get home quicker and had then left it.

"Besides, the driver was a good friend of mine. I assured them that it was all right."

" 'No,' they replied, 'you stole it.' Of course they were stumped about just how or where I stole it.

"It's funny, I once really did commit a crime. I should have been sent here long ago. But that time I got away with it. Now they've sent me here for nothing at all—

[6]*The Lives of the Saints* is a four-volume book written by Alban Butler (1711-1773), an English priest.

"Ah, well, I admit I'm lying. I've been in Siberia before. But I did not stay long."

"Where are you from?" someone asked.

"Vladimir. That's where my family is from. My name is Makar; they call me Semyonich too."

Ivan lifted his head and asked, "Tell me, Makar, do you know the merchant family Aksionov of Vladimir? Are they still alive?"

"Know them? Sure I do. The Aksionovs are wealthy, though their father is in Siberia. He's just a sinner like us, it seems!

"What about you, Grandpa? How did you get here?"

Ivan did not like to speak about his **tribulation**. Sighing, he merely replied, "For my sins I have been here for the last twenty-six years."

"What sins?" asked Makar Semyonich.

Ivan only said, "Well, well, I must have deserved it!"

He would have left it at that, but his companions told Ivan's history to the newcomers. They explained how someone had murdered a merchant and then planted the knife in Ivan's bag. As a result, innocent Ivan had been condemned.

Upon hearing this, Makar gazed at Ivan and slapped his own knee. He cried, "Well, this is amazing! Just amazing! But you've grown so old, Grandpa!"

The others asked Makar why he was so surprised and where he'd seen Ivan before.

However, Makar did not reply. He only **reiterated**, "It's amazing that we should meet here, boys!"

Makar's reaction made Ivan wonder if he knew who the real murderer was. So he said, "Maybe you've heard of my case before, Makar. Or maybe you've seen me before?"

"How could I help hearing about it? The world's full of gossip. But many years have passed since then, and I've forgotten what I heard."

"Perhaps you heard who really murdered the merchant?" Ivan pressed.

Makar laughed and replied, "It must have been the fellow who owned the bag where the knife was found! Because if anyone else hid the knife there—well, as the saying goes, 'He's not a thief till he's caught.' How could someone put a knife into your bag while you were dozing on top of it? It would surely have wakened you."

When Ivan heard this, he became convinced that Makar was the real murderer. He got up and walked away.

Ivan lay awake all that night. He felt deeply unhappy, and all sorts of visions floated before him.

He saw the image of his wife as she looked when he left her to go to the fair. She seemed so real that he felt he could reach out and touch her. Her face and her eyes danced before him. He heard her speak and laugh.

Then he saw his children. They were quite small, as they had been twenty-six years ago. One wore a little cloak. Another was still nursing at his mother's breast.

And then he **reminisced** about himself as he once was— young and lighthearted. He remembered how he sat playing the guitar at the inn where he was arrested. How free from worry he had been then!

In his mind, he pictured the place where he was whipped. He saw the executioner and the crowd pressing around. The chains, the convicts, the entire twenty-six years of his prison life, and his **premature** old age. Memories of all these things flooded over him. They made him so **despondent** that he felt like taking his life.

"And it's all because of that villain!" thought Ivan. His hatred against Makar grew so strong that he longed for revenge. He would have been willing to die for it himself.

All night long he prayed. Yet he could not find peace. During the day he could not go near Makar or even look at him.

Two weeks passed like this. Ivan could not sleep at night. His misery was so overwhelming that he did not know what to do.

One night as he walked about the prison he noticed some dirt come rolling out from under one of the prisoner's bunks. Ivan stopped to investigate.

Suddenly Makar Semyonich crept out from under the bunk. With an anxious face, he stared up at Ivan.

Ivan tried to move on without looking at him. But Makar grabbed his hand. He quickly told Ivan that he was digging a tunnel under the wall. He said he **disposed** of the dirt by sticking it in his boots. Then he emptied it out on the road daily when the prisoners were driven to work.

"Just keep quiet about this, old man, and you can escape too. If you rat on me, they may whip me to death, but I'll kill you first."

Ivan shook with anger as he glared at his enemy. Drawing back his hand, he said, "I do not want to escape, and you have no need to kill me. You killed me years ago!

"As to telling about your plan—I may or may not do it. It is in God's hands."

Next day, when the convicts were led to work, the soldiers noticed that some prisoner had emptied dirt out of his boots. The prison was searched and the tunnel found.

The Governor came and interrogated all the prisoners to find out who had planned the escape. They all swore they knew nothing about it. Those who did know would not betray Makar. They realized he would be whipped almost to death.

At last the Governor came to Ivan, whom he knew to be an **upright** man. The Governor said, "You are a truthful old man. So tell me, in God's name, who dug the tunnel?"

Makar Semyonich stood with a confident air, looking at the Governor and hardly even glancing at Ivan.

Ivan's lips and hands quaked. For a long time he stood silent, not able to speak a word. He thought, "Why should I protect one who has ruined my life? Let him pay for the pain I've suffered.

"But if I tell, they'll probably whip him to death. And

maybe my suspicions are false. After all, what good would it do me?''

"Well, old man," urged the Governor, "come, tell me. Who has been tunneling under the wall?"

With a glance at Makar, Ivan replied, "I cannot say, your honor. It is not God's will that I should tell. Do what you want to me. I am in your power."

The Governor **incessantly** pressed Ivan. But he would say nothing. The matter had to be dropped for the time being.

That night when Ivan was in bed and just dozing off, someone quietly approached and sat down beside him. Ivan peered through the darkness and recognized Makar.

"What more can you want from me?" asked Ivan. "Why are you here?"

Makar remained silent, so Ivan arose and said, "What do you want? Go away, or I'll call the guard!"

Makar bent near Ivan and whispered, "Please, Ivan, forgive me!"

"What for?" asked Ivan.

"I was the one who killed the merchant and hid the knife in your bag. I meant to kill you too, but I heard a noise outside. So I hid the knife in your bag and escaped out of the window."

Ivan was silent. He did not know what to say.

Makar slid off the bunk and kneeled before him. "Ivan," said he, "please forgive me! For the love of God, forgive me! I will confess that I was the one who murdered the merchant. You will be freed and allowed to go home."

"That's very easily said," said Ivan, "but I've suffered for your crime the last twenty-six years. Where could I go now? My wife is surely dead; my children have forgotten me. There's no place left for me."

Still kneeling, Makar beat his head on the floor. "Ivan, forgive me!" he cried. "Being beaten was not as painful as seeing you now. Yet you pitied me and did not tell. For Christ's sake, forgive me, though I'm nothing but a wretch!" And he began to weep.

Hearing Makar's sobs, Ivan began to weep too. "God will forgive you!" said he. "I may be a hundred times worse than you."

Even as he spoke these words his heart grew lighter. The desire for home left him. He no longer wished to leave the prison. He only hoped that his life would end.

Despite what Ivan had said, Makar Semyonich confessed his crime. But by the time the release order arrived, Ivan Aksionov was already dead.

"God Sees the Truth, but Waits" was first published in 1872.

INSIGHTS INTO
LEO TOLSTOY

(1828-1910)

Tolstoy was born in the Tula province of Russia.

Tolstoy was a true male chauvinist. He had strict ideas about a wife's duties. He thought she should bear children, raise them, and educate them. She also should run the household and totally support her husband.

Theory often runs into problems when tested in the real world. It's a well-known fact that Tolstoy had a very stormy marriage.

In 1851 Tolstoy enlisted in the Russian army. He was stationed at Sevastopol on the front line during the Crimean War. There he wrote his grim *Sevastopol Sketches*.

The sketches were an instant success. Even Czar Alexander II read them and admired Tolstoy's talent.

Soon after, special orders were issued to remove Tolstoy from the dangerous front line. The Czar obviously did not want to risk gaining a soldier at the expense of losing a great writer.

Tolstoy hated to spend money on himself. He often chose to walk great distances rather than take the train. He was known to hike up to 130 miles to get where he wanted.

Tolstoy found walking a pleasant habit as well. He loved fresh air and chatting with the lower classes.

The fact that Tolstoy was a light traveler eased his way. Even on long trips he only took with him a bit of food, a notebook and pencil, two pairs of socks, handkerchiefs, a change of clothes, and a bottle of stomach medicine.

Tolstoy formed some interesting ideas about education and wanted to test them. So he built his own school and invited peasant children to come.

Tolstoy's teaching methods were very unusual. He got rid of the grading system at once. He did not believe children should be punished or rewarded for their classwork.

Moreover, he felt students should want to learn—not be forced or tricked into it. School should draw out the knowledge already inside the child, he declared.

Tolstoy's experiment did not last long. The school closed after having proved "impractical."

Tolstoy's wife, Sonya, was also his secretary. Night after night, she sat up late copying what Tolstoy had written that day. This was no simple task. Tolstoy's tiny script was most easily read with a microscope.

Besides Sonya's knack for decoding what no one else could, she was also telepathic. She could guess at the meaning of unfinished sentences, words, and notes.

Her talents were priceless. During the six years Tolstoy took to write *War and Peace,* Sonya copied the work seven times.

Other works by Tolstoy:
"The Death of Ivan Ilych," short story
Anna Karenina, book
Confession, book
The Cossacks, book
Resurrection, book

A PIECE OF STRING

GUY DE MAUPASSANT

VOCABULARY PREVIEW

Below is a list of words that appear in the story. Read the list and get to know the words before you start the story.

abashed—embarrassed or confused
accomplice—partner or assistant in crime
bantering—teasing; joking
confronted—faced, usually boldly or bravely
disquieted—uneasy; anxious
distraught—distressed and troubled
enveloped—wrapped
illiterate—unable to read
impassive—emotionless
incredulous—questioning or unbelieving
indignation—anger over an injustice or insult
intricate—complex and elaborate
mulled—thought over; considered
obese—overweight; fat
poultry—birds, such as chickens and turkeys, raised for meat or eggs
reaping—gathering or harvesting
robust—strong and healthy
salvation—the state of being saved from evil or damnation
throng—crowd
vendor—seller; peddler

A PIECE OF STRING

"Waste not, want not" is a little saying that Hauchecome lives by. And who can tell how the piece of string he finds might come in handy? It would make a good cord for a package or a fine fastener for a gate. Even a noose for an innocent man.

It was market day in Goderville. Along all the roads nearby came the peasants and their wives.

The men made their way with slow steps. Their whole bodies bent forward at each stride they took with their long twisted legs. They had been deformed by hard work and by pushing heavy plows. At the same time, this labor had raised their left shoulders and twisted their trunks.

GUY DE MAUPASSANT

Reaping wheat had also left them bowlegged. This was because they were in the habit of steadying themselves to take a firm stand.

Their blue shirts were stiffly starched and shone as if waxed. Little designs in white at the neck and wrists decorated them.

These shirts puffed about their bony bodies, like balloons ready to carry them off. From each shirt a head, two arms, and two feet stuck out.

Some led a cow or a calf by a cord. Their wives followed behind the animal. The wives often whipped the cow's rear with a leafy branch to speed it up.

The wives also carried large baskets on their arms. Chickens or ducks thrust their heads out over the rim.

The women walked with a quicker, brisker step than their mates. Their slim straight figures were wrapped in thin little shawls pinned across their flat breasts. Their heads were **enveloped** in white cloths fixed atop the hair. Caps set upon the cloths.

A wagon passed, going at the speed of a nag's jerky trot and shaking strangely. Two men were seated side by side. A woman sat in the bottom of the vehicle. She held onto the sides of the wagon to brace herself against the hard jolts.

In the public square of Goderville there was a crowd. Both human beings and animals mixed together in this **throng**. The horns of cattle, the tall hats of rich peasants, and the caps of peasant women rose above the crowd.

The noisy, shrill, screaming voices made a continual and savage racket. Sometimes you could hear a farmer's **robust** laugh or the long mooing of a cow.

The crowd smacked of the stable, the dairy and dirt pile, hay and sweat. It had that unpleasant odor, both human and animal, that is unique to the people of the field.

Maitre[1] Hauchecome of Breaute had just arrived at

[1]Maitre means master or mister.

Goderville. He was making his way toward the public square when he saw a little piece of string on the ground.

Hauchecome, who was as thrifty as any true Norman,[2] thought that anything of use should be picked up. So he bent down painfully—for he had rheumatism.[3] He took the bit of thin string from the ground and began to roll it carefully.

Just then he noticed Maitre Malandain, the harness maker. Malandain was standing at his door looking at him.

Before this, the two men had had words about a halter. They were now on bad terms since both were good at hating.

Hauchecome was seized with shame to have his enemy see him picking a bit of string out of the dirt. He quickly hid his find under his shirt, then in his pants' pocket. Then he pretended to be still searching the ground for something which he did not find.

At last he went toward the market. He kept his head bowed, bent even further forward by his pain.

He was soon lost in the loud, slow-moving crowd which was busy with their endless bargaining. The peasants wandered back and forth. They were perplexed, always in fear of being cheated.

Not wanting to risk a decision, they watched the **vendor's** eye. Always the peasants were trying to discover the trick in the man and the flaw in the beast.

Placing their huge baskets at their feet, the women took out the **poultry**. The birds, with terrified eyes and scarlet crests, were displayed. They lay upon the ground with their feet tied together.

The women would listen to offers. Then they would give their price in a dry voice and with an **impassive** face.

---

[2]A Norman is a descendant of Viking raiders. These Vikings conquered parts of France and then spread to other parts of Europe.

[3]Rheumatism is a condition that causes pain and stiffness in the nerves, muscles, or bones.

Sometimes they would suddenly decide to agree to some lower price. At such times they would shout to a customer who was slowly walking away, "All right, Maitre Authirne. I'll give it to you for that."

Little by little the square was deserted. The Angelus[4] rang at noon. Those who had stayed too long scattered to their shops.

At Jourdain's the big room was full of people eating. The large courtyard outside was full, too. It was thronged with vehicles of all kinds. Carts, gigs, wagons, and dump carts were packed into it.

Most of the vehicles were yellow with dirt and mended and patched. Some lifted their shafts heavenwards like two arms. Others had their shafts plunged to the ground, their backs in the air.

The diners sat at a large table. Just across from them was an immense fireplace. It brimmed with bright flames and cast a warm heat on the backs of those sitting on the bench nearby.

Three spits were turning in the fire. Chickens, pigeons, and legs of mutton were roasting on them. An appetizing odor of roast beef and gravy, dripping over nicely browned skin, came from the hearth. The smell increased the merry mood and made everybody's mouth water.

All the well-to-do peasants ate at Maitre Jourdain's tavern. Jourdain, innkeeper and horse dealer, was a rascal who had money.

Dishes were passed and emptied, as were jugs of golden cider. Everyone spoke about his affairs, his buys and sales. They discussed the crops. Green things should do well in this weather, but not the wheat.

Suddenly a drum roll was heard in the court outside the tavern. Everybody except a few uninterested people ran for

---

[4]Angelus is a bell that rings at certain times during the day to summon Roman Catholics to prayer.

the door or the windows. They were still chewing their last bites and held their napkins in their hands.

After the announcer had ceased beating his drum, he called out in a jerky voice, "This announcement is for citizens of Goderville and all persons at the market.

"A wallet was lost this morning between nine and ten o'clock on the road to Benzeville. This black leather wallet contained five hundred francs,[5] as well as some business papers.

"The finder is requested to return this wallet at once to the mayor's office or Maitre Fortune Houlbreque of Manneville. A reward of twenty francs is offered."

Then the man went away. The heavy roll of the drum and his voice were heard again at a distance.

The diners began to talk about this announcement. They **mulled** over the chances of Maitre Houlbreque's finding his wallet. And in this fashion the meal drew to a close.

They were just finishing their coffee when a police chief appeared at the door. He asked, "Is Maitre Hauchecome of Breaute here?"

Hauchecome, seated at the far end of the table, spoke up. "Here I am."

The officer continued. "Maitre Hauchecome, will you kindly go with me to the mayor's office? The mayor would like to speak with you."

The peasant, surprised and upset, swallowed in one gulp his tiny glass of brandy. Then he rose, even more bent than he had been in the morning. After a rest, the first steps were always painful.

Hauchecome set out with the officer. He continued to repeat, "Here I am, here I am."

The mayor, seated in a chair, was awaiting Hauchecome.

[5]The franc is a piece of French currency.

He was the notary[6] of the district. An **obese**, serious man, he spoke in a self-important way.

"Maitre Hauchecome," he said, "you were seen picking up Maitre Houlbreque's wallet this morning."

The astonished countryman looked at the mayor. This suspicion that rested on him without his knowing why already terrified him.

"Me? Me? Me pick up the wallet?"

"Yes, you, yourself."

"I swear, I never heard of it."

"But you were seen."

"I was seen? Me? Who says he saw me?"

"Maitre Malandain, the harness maker."

Then the old man remembered. He understood and flushed with anger.

"Ah, he saw me, the old clodhopper. He saw me pick up this string here, Monsieur[7] Mayor."

Rummaging in his pocket, he pulled out the piece of string.

But the mayor was **incredulous** and shook his head.

"You cannot expect me to believe that Maitre Malandain—who is a trustworthy man—thought this string was a wallet."

The furious peasant lifted his hand. He spat to prove the truth of his word. "Nevertheless, it is God's truth, the sacred truth, Monsieur Mayor. I swear it by my soul and my **salvation**."

The mayor went on. "After picking up the object, you stood like a block of wood, scanning the mud for a long time. You were searching for any money that had fallen out."

The good old man choked with **indignation** and fear.

"How anyone can tell—how anyone can tell—such lies

---

[6]A notary is a public official who certifies documents.

[7]Monsieur means sir or gentleman.

to ruin an honest man's reputation! How can anyone—"

He protested in vain. No one believed him. Monsieur Malandain **confronted** him and testified. The harness maker repeated his story and stood by it. They swore at each other for an hour.

Then, at his own request, Maitre Hauchecome was searched. Nothing was found on him.

Finally the perplexed mayor released him with a warning. The mayor said he would discuss the case with the public prosecutor[8] and ask for further orders.

The news had spread. As he left the mayor's office, the old man was surrounded. People questioned him with a serious or **bantering** curiosity. As yet there was no indignation in their questions.

He began to tell how he found the string. But no one believed him. In fact, they laughed at him.

Hauchecome moved on, stopping his friends along the way. Time and again he stated his case, made his protests. He would turn his pockets inside out to prove he had nothing.

They said, "Go on, you old rascal!"

And he grew furious. He was angry and **distraught** at not being believed. But, not knowing what to do, he kept repeating his story.

Night fell. He had to leave. He headed home with three neighbors to whom he showed the spot where he picked up the string. All along the road he told of his adventure.

In the evening he took a walk in the village of Breaute in order to tell everyone of his experience. He only met with incredulity.

He was ill that night because of it.

About one o'clock in the afternoon the next day, the wallet and its contents were returned to Maitre Houlbreque. Marius Paumelle, a hired man in the service of Maitre Breton

---

[8]A public prosecutor is a lawyer who is in charge of representing the government in court cases.

(a farmer at Ymanville), was the one who returned it.

This man claimed to have found the object in the road. Being **illiterate**, he had carried it to the house and turned it over to his employer.

The news spread through the area. Maitre Hauchecome was told about it. He immediately went through the town, relating his story with its happy climax. He was triumphant.

"What distressed me so much was not the thing itself as the lying. There is nothing so shameful as to be placed under a cloud because of a lie."

He talked of his adventure all day. He told it on the road to people passing by. He went to the tavern and cornered the people drinking there. And he spoke to persons coming out of church the following Sunday. He even stopped strangers to tell them.

He was calm again. Yet something **disquieted** him without his knowing exactly what it was. People seemed to listen to him with amusement. They did not seem convinced. He began to feel that remarks were being made behind his back.

On Tuesday of the next week he went to the Goderville market. He went simply because he felt the urge to discuss his case.

Malandain, standing at his door, began laughing when he saw him pass. Why?

He approached a farmer from Crequetot. But this man would not let him finish. Instead, he thumped Hauchecome in the stomach and said, "You big rascal."

Then he turned his back on Hauchecome.

Hauchecome was **abashed**. Why had he been called a big rascal?

When he sat down at a table in Jourdain's tavern, he began to explain "the incident."

A horse dealer from Monvilliers called to him. "Come, come, old trickster. That's an old game. I know all about you and your piece of string!"

Hauchecome stammered, "But, after all, the wallet was found—"

The other man replied, "Shut up, old fellow. There's one that finds and one that turns it in. At any rate you're mixed up in it somehow."

The peasant stood up choking. He understood. He was being accused of having a partner, an **accomplice**, return the wallet.

He tried to protest. But the whole table began to laugh.

He could not finish his dinner. So he left, followed by jeers.

He returned home ashamed and indignant. He felt even more dejected because his Norman cunning made him capable of doing what they suspected. And he would boast about it, too.

In a confused way, he realized that it was impossible to prove his innocence. His cleverness was too well known. And he was heartbroken by the unjust suspicion.

Then he began to relate the tale again. He lengthened the story each day. And each day he added new reasons, more fiery protests, and more solemn oaths.

He prepared these additions in his hours alone. His whole mind had now surrendered to the story of the string. But as his defense grew more **intricate**, his arguments more clever, he was believed less and less.

"Those are the excuses of a liar," they said behind his back.

He felt it. He ate his heart out over it. He wore himself out with vain attempts. He wasted away before their very eyes.

The jokers now made him tell about the string for amusement. He was coaxed like a soldier who has been at war is asked to tell of his battles. His mind, shaken to the core, began to weaken.

Near the end of December, he took to his bed.

He died in the early part of January. In a feverish fit just before his death, he kept claiming his innocence. Over and over he repeated, "A piece of string, a piece of string. Look, here it is, Monsieur Mayor."

"A Piece of String" was first published in 1889.

INSIGHTS INTO
GUY DE MAUPASSANT
(1850-1893)

Maupassant was born in Normandy, France.

Maupassant had a pressing need to see things exactly as they were. Naturally he hated the masks most people hid behind. He felt the writer's task was to reveal—if just for an instant—the truth beneath the mask.

Maupassant spared only prostitutes and peasants. He felt they did not pretend to be other than what they were.

Soon after his second story was published, Maupassant's life took a happy turn. He was able to quit his job as clerk and write full time.

But even while a clerk, Maupassant did not let his job interfere with his wish to become a writer. In fact, his dull job actually inspired him. He wrote many tales about the clerk's constant struggle to keep up appearances.

Maupassant became a pupil of writer Gustave Flaubert. He gladly accepted Flaubert's criticisms and high standards. In fact, till Maupassant felt he'd mastered his craft, he himself threw away story after story.

"Ball of Fat," Maupassant's second printed tale, marked the peak of the ten-year relationship. It was the first story by Maupassant that Flaubert called brilliant.

Two weeks after the story appeared, Flaubert died. Devoted Maupassant was the one who prepared Flaubert's body for burial.

continued

Maupassant suffered from syphilis for half of his life. In 1891 the disease finally overcame him. His depressions grew worse and his hallucinations increased.

The author was convinced he was losing his mind. He tried to commit suicide twice.

Two years later, he died in a Paris asylum.

Other works by Maupassant:
"The Heritage," short story
"The House of Mme. Tellier," short story
"Mademoiselle Fifi," short story
"The Necklace," short story
"The Story of a Farm Girl," short story
Bel Ami, book

THE DIARY OF A MADMAN
NIKOLAI GOGOL

VOCABULARY PREVIEW

Below is a list of words that appear in the story. Read the list and get to know the words before you start the story.

antiquated—old-fashioned; outdated
apt—likely
commotion—uproar and confusion
delegate—representative; spokesperson
deteriorates—decays; worsens
inane—silly or foolish; senseless
incognito—with one's identity hidden
infernal—damned or cursed; also, relating to hell
intrigue—secret plot or scheme
lackey—a servant or follower, especially one who is *servile* (see definition below)
licentious—ignoring rules of morality and following one's own sexual desires; immoral
lunacy—madness
oblivious—unaware or unconscious of
prestige—importance and influence
servile—overly obedient; crawling at someone's feet
stench—stink
supplicant—one who humbly pleads for aid
sustenance—food or nourishment
tier—row, as in a *tier* of seats at a stadium
vile—disgusting; nasty

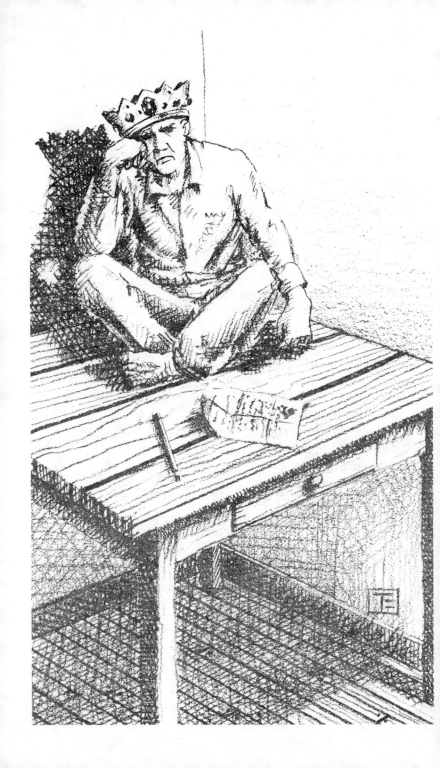

THE
DIARY
OF A
MADMAN

He may look content sharpening his quills, but Aksentii hates his job. His only interests at work are promotions and his boss's daughter.

Aksentii has a rare talent that may deliver him from this boring world. He can see and hear what others cannot. He can tell you the secret thoughts of two little dogs. Or if you're interested in knowing the name of the next king of Spain . . .

OCTOBER 3

Something unusual happened today.

I woke up quite late. When Marva brought in my clean shoes, I asked her what time it was. When I heard that it was long past ten, I quickly put on my clothes.

Really, I must admit I'd rather not have gone

NIKOLAI GOGOL

to the office at all. I could picture the ugly look my department head would give me.

He's been saying to me for the longest time, "Why are you always in such a muddle? You dash around sometimes like a crazy man. Your work is often in an awful tangle. Not even the devil could straighten it out. You're **apt** to begin a title without capitalizing and not give a date or reference number."

The spiteful old bird! He must envy me because I sit in the director's room and sharpen his quills.

Given all this, I would have stayed home if I hadn't wanted to see the cashier. I had hoped to try to squeeze just a tiny advance on my salary from that Jew.[1]

That man is unbelievable! It would have to be the Day of Judgment before he'd give you a month's wages in advance. You can be at your rope's end and beg until you rot. But he still won't budge, the old devil.

Yet I hear that his own cook slaps him at home. Everyone says it's true.

I cannot see any advantage in working in our department. No fringe benefits at all.

You can't begin to compare it to working for the city office or the treasury, for instance. There you can spot a clerk parked in a corner, scribbling away with his pen. He may be dressed in a tattered coat and have a face that makes you want to spit. Yet just take a look at the country house he rents!

Don't even dare to present him with a gold-covered china cup. He'd say, "That may do for a doctor, but—" But for him—nothing less than a pair of racehorses or a carriage. Or a fur that comes to about three hundred rubles.[2]

Oh, he seems so quiet and acts so polite and **servile**. He'll say, "Would you please loan me your penknife so I can

---

[1] Aksentii reveals many such prejudices throughout the story.
[2] The ruble is the basis of the Russian currency.

sharpen my quill?''

But he'll strip the very clothes off a **supplicant's** back, down to the shirt.

Yet I'll admit that it's more elegant working for our department. The cleanliness of our place can't even be imagined by those in the city office. And we have red mahogany tables and our superiors always use the polite form of address.

Yes, it's the elegance that keeps me there. Without that, I admit I'd have left the department long ago.

I got out my old overcoat. It was pouring buckets, so I also grabbed my umbrella.

The streets were almost empty. The only people in sight were some peasant women with their skirts draped over their heads, some merchants with umbrellas, and a few coachmen.

As for people of breeding, there was only one of my fellow civil servants. I spotted him at a street corner.

As soon as I saw him, I said to myself, "I know you're not going to the office, my brother. You're dogging that girl ahead of you. And it's her legs you're eyeing."

What a rascal the civil servant is! In matters like this, he can get the better of an army officer any day. The civil servant will go after anything so long as it's wearing a bonnet.

Just as I was thinking this, a carriage pulled up in front of a store I was passing. I recognized at once that the carriage belonged to the director of our department.

But what can he need here, I wondered. No, it must be his daughter.

I flattened myself against the wall. The footman opened the door of the carriage, and she fluttered out like a little bird.

How she glanced about! First right, then left. How her eyes and eyebrows flashed!

Oh God, I'm lost, lost forever. And why did she come out driving in this rain? Just try and argue after this that women aren't crazy about clothes.

She didn't recognize me. Besides, I was trying to wrap myself up. You see, my coat was quite filthy and **antiquated** too. These days the fashion is for long coat collars. I had two very short ones, one lapped over the other. And the material was not waterproof.

Her little dog did not move fast enough to get into the store. The animal was forced to remain outside.

I know this little dog. They call her Madgie.

Then, about a minute later, I heard a piping little voice. "Hello, Madgie."

My God, who said that?

I turned and saw two ladies strolling under their umbrellas. One was old. Her companion was young and pretty.

They had already passed by when again I heard, right next to me, "Shame on you, Madgie!"

What on earth was happening? I saw Madgie and a dog that had been trailing the two ladies sniffing at one another.

"Oh," I said to myself, "I must be drunk. Yet that's not too likely since it doesn't happen very often."

"Oh no, Fidele, you're wrong." With my own eyes, I saw Madgie say the words.

"I was—bow wow—I was—bow wow wow—very ill."

Some kind of a pet dog! I confess I was quite taken aback to hear her speak.

Later, however, when I had time to think it all through, I was no longer amazed. In fact, the world has seen many such things before.

I understand that, in England, a fish surfaced and said a few words in a strange language. Scholars have been trying to work out just what it said for three years. So far, they haven't figured it out.

I've also read in the newspapers about two cows. They went into a store and requested a pound of tea.

Despite this, I must confess I was much more stunned when Madgie said, "I swear I wrote you, Fidele. Perhaps Polkan didn't deliver my letter."

I'd be willing to bet a month's pay that I've never heard of a dog that could write. Anyway, only a nobleman can write properly.

Of course, there are some merchants or traders who can scribble—even peasants. But their kind of writing is mechanical. Commas, periods, style—none of that for them.

Therefore, I was surprised. I must confess that lately I've been seeing and hearing some very strange, unheard of things.

I said to myself, "Well, I'll follow this dog. I'll find out who she is and what she thinks."

I opened my umbrella and followed the ladies. We crossed Pea Street. From there we went on to Merchant's Road. Then we turned down Carpenter's Avenue and finally stopped at a large building close to Cuckoo Bridge.

"I know this house," I said to myself. "It belongs to Zverkov."

What a dump it is! You can find all sorts there. It's overflowing with crooks and foreigners.

And my fellow civil servants pack the place. They live like dogs, crowding on top of one another. One of my friends—a good trumpet player—lives there too.

The ladies went up to the fifth floor.

"Good," I thought. "I won't follow them in now. I'll just make a note of the address and come back at my first chance."

OCTOBER 4

Today is Wednesday, so I was in the director's study. I deliberately came early and sharpened all the quills.

The director must be a very clever man. His study is packed with bookcases. I read some of the titles. Such scholarly learning all over the place! It leaves the common person totally behind. The books are all in French or German.

Just look into his face. My heavens! How the importance gleams from his eyes!

I've never heard him speak one trivial word. Apart from the times, maybe, when you give him some papers. Then he might say, "How's the weather today?" "It's rather damp, sir."

Yes, he's a breed apart from our class. The true statesman! Still, I notice he has a special fondness for me.

If only his daughter . . . Oh, I'm such a rascal! Well, never mind, never mind . . . Hush!

I was reading the *Bee*.[3] The French are really a stupid people, aren't they? Just what do they want? By heaven, I'd like to give every one of them a good beating.

I also read a nice account of a ball by a landowner from Kursk. Kursk landowners really do write well.

Then I noticed it was twelve-thirty. Yet our director still hadn't come out of his bedroom.

Then, an hour later, something happened that no one could properly capture with pen. The door opened. Thinking it was the director, I leaped up from my desk with the documents in my hand.

But it was her, in person!

Holy Fathers, how she was dressed! Her gown was white and quite feathery, like a swan. When she looked at me, I could have sworn she was the sun!

She nodded to me and asked, "Has Papa been in here?"

Ah, such a voice! A canary, a living, breathing canary.

"Madam," I wanted to say, "don't order me put to death. But if that is what you decide, may you strike me down with your own noble hand."

However, my tongue would not obey me. I could only mumble, "No, madam."

---

[3]The *Northern Bee* was a journal that attacked famous writers of the day, including Gogol. The *Bee* was secretly protected by the police.

She glanced from me to the books. Then she dropped her handkerchief. I rushed like a fiend and slipped on the damned wooden floor. I nearly broke my nose. But I managed to regain my balance and picked up the handkerchief.

By the saints, what a hanky! Such fine, delicate linen—and perfumed, sweet perfume. You could almost smell the fine breeding.

She thanked me and smiled. But it was such a faint smile that her sweet lips scarcely moved. Then she went out.

I went back to my seat and stayed there. When an hour had passed, a servant entered. He announced, "You may leave, Aksentii Ivanovitch. The master has already gone out."

One thing I cannot tolerate is a **lackey**. You'll always find them lazing in the entryway. They don't even bother to honor me with the smallest nod.

Besides that, one of these clods once dared to offer me some snuff. And he didn't even bother to get up! You idiots, don't you realize that I'm a civil servant and come from a noble family?

I fetched my hat and put on my overcoat myself—without help, of course. Then I left. Those fellows wouldn't dream of lending you a hand!

At home I lay on my bed for a while. Then I copied a wonderful verse.

Without you one hour died
As slowly as a year.
"What is my life worth," I cried,
"When you are not here?"

Sounds like something by Pushkin.[4]

---

[4]Alexander Pushkin (1799-1837) is a Russian poet and short story writer.

That evening, I put on my overcoat and walked to my ladyship's home. I waited by the gate a long time to see if she would come out and get into her carriage. But she never did.

NOVEMBER 6

My chief is in an ugly mood. When I got to the office, he summoned me and started this conversation.

"Well now, tell me. What are you after?"

"What do you mean? I'm not after anything," I answered.

"Come on, try to understand. You're over forty. At that age, you should have more sense. Just who do you imagine you are? You think you're hiding anything from me? I know you're after the director's daughter.

"But take a long look at yourself," he continued. What are you? Nothing, a real nobody. You haven't a penny. And take a look in the mirror. How dare you consider something like that?"

Damn him! He's got a face like a medicine bottle. And that little twist of hair on his head is all curled and oiled . . .

Because he holds his head so high, he thinks he can do as he pleases.

I know what's at the bottom of his lecture. He's jealous of me. He's probably seen how favors have been showered on me in the office.

As if I cared what he thinks. So what if he's a court official! So he shows off his gold watch chain and has his boots specially made for thirty rubles. Damn him anyway!

Does he think my father was a mere merchant or a tailor or a common military man? Well, I'm a gentleman!

I could be promoted anytime, as well. I'm only forty-two. Your career is actually just beginning at that age.

Just you wait, my friend. I'll rise higher than you some day. With God's grace, I'll go much, much higher. I'll end up in a position beyond your imagination.

You think you're the only one with **prestige**? Just give me a fashionable new coat and a tie like yours. Then you wouldn't be fit to shine my shoes. No money—that's my only problem.

NOVEMBER 8

Went to the theater. The play was about that Russian fool Filatka. I laughed a lot. There was a vaudeville show too, with funny lines mocking lawyers.

The verses were so outrageous that I wondered how they ever passed the censor.[5] They clearly stated that merchants cheat everybody. And they said that the merchants' sons are **licentious** and try to butt their way into society.

There was a funny couplet[6] as well. It complained about how journalists tear down everything. The author begged for the audience to shield him from the press.

Dramatists write quite entertaining plays these days. I like going to plays. Whenever I can scrape together a little change, I go. I can't help it.

But civil servants are such pigs. Those fools go to the theater? Not likely. No, not even if the tickets were free.

One actress sang very well . . . She reminded me of . . .

Oh, I'm such a rascal! Never mind, never mind . . . Hush!

NOVEMBER 9

I left for the office at eight. The chief pretended he didn't see me come in. I also behaved as if nothing had changed between us.

I leafed through the papers and sorted them. Left at four.

Passed the director's section, but didn't see anyone.

After dinner, lay on my bed most of the time.

---

[5]Censors decide if performances, art, books, etc., may appear in public. Usually they judge a work on the basis of political or moral content.
[6]A couplet is a rhyming verse of two lines.

NOVEMBER 11

Today I sat in the director's study. Sharpened twenty-three quills for him, and for her . . . Oh my, four quills.

He wants as many quills handy as possible. He really must be brilliant! He doesn't talk much as a rule. I guess he must be thinking over everything in that brain. I wish I knew what's on his mind most of the time—what's brewing in there.

I wish I could get a real glimpse of these people—how they live, with all their clever remarks and courtly jokes. I'd like to know how they act and what they do when they're with their own kind.

I've often tried to strike up a conversation with the director. But I'm damned if it's ever worked. I say it's warm or cold today and then come to a dead stop.

Just once I'd like to peep inside their drawing room. Most of the time you just see the open door and maybe a second door leading to another room.

Oh, you should see the fine decorations! Mirrors and fine china galore!

I'd love to see her room too. Yes, I'd really like to go there! Just to peep into her bedroom. See all her tiny jars and bottles planted there amid those flowers that you don't even dare breathe on. To see the dress she's just taken off lying there, looking more like air than a dress.

How wonderful it would be to have a peak into her bedroom! What wonders must be inside there. It's paradise, better than heaven.

What I wouldn't give to see the little stool her dainty foot steps upon when she gets out of bed. Then watch how she pulls a wonderfully fine, white stocking over that foot . . .

Oh, never mind, never mind . . . Hush!

But today an idea suddenly came to me when I recalled the conversation between the two dogs on Nevsky Avenue.

"Good," I thought, "now I'll find out everything. I'll

just get the letters of those wretched mutts. I know I'll discover something.''

Now I'll admit that once I called Madgie and said to her, ''All right, Madgie, we're alone now. If you wish, I'll even bolt the door so that no one will see us.

''Now, tell me whatever you know about your mistress: what she's like and all that. I swear I'll not repeat a thing to anyone.''

But the sly little dog just put her tail between her legs, slunk down, and left the room in silence. It was as though she hadn't heard a thing.

For a long time I've suspected that dogs are much more clever than people. I was even certain they could speak and simply chose not to out of stubbornness. A dog is a remarkable politician. It notices everything, every step you take.

Still, whatever happens, tomorrow I'll go to Zverkov's house. I'll question Fidele. If possible, I'll lay my hands on Madgie's letters to her.

NOVEMBER 12

At two this afternoon I went out, determined to find Fidele and question her. I can't stand the smell of cabbage which comes pouring out of all the shops along Merchant's Road. This and the **infernal** smell pouring from under the gates of every house sent me running, holding my nose.

And those disgusting shopkeepers send so much soot and smoke from their shops! It's not a fit place for a well-bred person to take a stroll.

When I reached the sixth floor and rang the bell, out came a girl with little freckles. She wasn't too bad looking at that.

I recognized her at once. She was the one I'd seen strolling with the old woman.

She blushed a little. I immediately saw that what she needed was a boyfriend.

"What do you want?" she asked.

"I want to have a talk with your dog," I said.

The girl was stupid—I saw that at once.

At that moment the dog ran in yapping at me. As I was trying to grab her, the nasty creature almost bit my nose.

But then I saw her basket in the corner. That's what I wanted!

I went over to it and searched through the straw. To my delight, I found a small bundle of papers. Seeing what I was up to, the nasty little beast first took a bite out of my calf. Then, when she sniffed around and found I'd taken her letters, she began whining and cozying up to me.

But I told her, "No, my dear. So long!" And off I went.

I believe the girl must have thought I was a madman. She seemed deeply frightened, indeed.

Once home, I wanted to set to work immediately. I hoped to have those letters sorted before dark since I can't see well by candlelight.

But Marva decided to scrub the floor just then. Those stupid Finns always fall into a passion for cleanliness at the worst times. So I went out for a walk to think over what had happened.

Now, finally, I'll understand their motives, uncover all the little details. I'll get to the bottom of everything.

Dogs are a clever race. They know all about **intrigue**. So everything's all sure to be in their letters. All there is to know about the director's character and actions will be there.

And she, there's sure to be something about her . . .

But never mind that . . . Hush!

I came home towards evening. Most of the time I lay on my bed.

NOVEMBER 13

Well, let's take a look now. This letter appears quite legible. Yet there *is* something doglike about the handwriting.

Let's read it:

Dear Fidele,

I still find I can't get accustomed to that common name of yours. Couldn't they find you a better one? Fidele, like Rose, is very commonplace.

But that's all beside the point. I'm very glad we have decided to write to each other.

The letter is very properly written. Even the punctuation and spelling are correct. This is much better than our department chief can do, though he claims to have studied at some university or other.

Let's see what else it says:

I believe that sharing thoughts and feelings with another is one of the main blessings in life.

Hm! That thought is stolen from a work translated from the German. The author's name has slipped my mind for the moment.

I speak from experience, though I've never been beyond the gates of our house. But then, isn't my life full of pleasures? My young mistress, whom Papa calls Sophie, is just wild about me.

Oh, oh! Never mind, never mind. Hush!

Papa often pets me too. I drink tea and coffee with cream. Oh, my dear, I must tell you that I don't see the attraction in those half-gnawed bones which our Polkan chews on in the kitchen.

I only like bones from game birds. Even then I'll only take them if the marrow hasn't been sucked out by someone else. A mix of sauces is nice as long as you don't add capers[7] or vegetables.

But what is most disgusting are those little pellets of bread. Some person sitting at the table—who has touched all sorts of filthy things—starts kneading a piece of bread with those same hands. Then he calls you and forces the pellet into your mouth.

To refuse would be bad manners. So you eat it, despite your disgust . . .

What's the meaning of all this? What rubbish! As though there weren't something better to write about. Let's look at the next page. Perhaps there will be something more interesting there.

Now, I'll happily tell you what goes on in this household. I've mentioned before the major figure in our house, whom Sophie calls Papa. He's a very strange man . . .

At last! Yes, I knew they were shrewd, whatever the topic. Let's see what she has to say about Papa.

. . . a very strange man. He's silent most of the time. He speaks very rarely. But a week ago he kept saying to himself, "Will I get it or not?"

Once he even asked me, "Well, Madgie, what do you think? Will I get it or won't I?"

I couldn't understand a bit of it. So I sniffed his shoe and left the room.

Then, my dear, a week later Papa came home absolutely delighted. All that morning people in uniform came and congratulated him.

At dinner Papa was merrier than I'd ever seen him. He told many little stories.

---

[7]Capers are the pickled flower buds of a shrub. They are sometimes added to sauces.

After dinner, he picked me up and held me as high as his shoulders. He said, "Look, Madgie, what's this?"

I saw some sort of a ribbon. I sniffed at it, but it had no odor whatever.

Finally, I slyly gave it a lick. It was a little salty.

Hm. This dog really goes too far. She should be whipped. So he's ambitious, is he? I must keep that in mind.

Good-bye, my dear. I must hurry and, etc., etc., etc. I'll finish this tomorrow.

Hello, I am back with you. Today my mistress, Sophie . . .

Aha! Let's see what she says about Sophie. I am such a devil! Never mind, never mind. Let's go on.

. . . my mistress, Sophie, was in a terrific fuss. She was getting ready for a ball. I was pleased, for this meant I'd have a chance to write to you.

Sophie is always very happy when she has a ball to go to. However, getting dressed for it usually makes her cross.

Personally, my dear, I can see no pleasure in going to a ball. Sophie usually returns home from balls at six in the morning. I can tell by her pale, tired face that the poor thing hasn't had a bite to eat.

I confess I could never live that kind of life. If I couldn't have game in sauce or chicken-wing stews, I don't know what would become of me. A sauce is tasty even with porridge. But nothing will help carrots, turnips, or artichokes . . .

The style is incredibly jerky. You can see that it's not written by a human being. It starts off all right and then **deteriorates** into dogginess.

Let's see another letter. Looks quite long. Hm, no date!

Oh, my dear, how deeply I feel the approach of spring. My heart beats as though it were waiting for something. There's a constant hum in my ears. Often I stand at the doors, listening intently for several minutes.

I must confess, I have plenty of suitors. I often sit by the window and watch them.

If only you knew how ugly some of them are. There's one wretched mongrel with stupidity written all over his face. He swaggers along the street and imagines he's someone very important. He's so sure everyone will admire him. I paid no attention to him, just as if I hadn't even noticed him.

Then you should see the terrifying Great Dane that stops in front of my window! If he stood up on his hind legs— which the clod probably can't even manage—he would be a head taller than Sophie's Papa. And Papa is quite tall himself, as well as fat.

That stupid Great Dane seems very bold. I growled at him, but he didn't even blink. He just hung his tongue out, let his huge ears droop, and kept gazing at my window. The oaf!

But, my dear, you don't really imagine that I'm cold to all who come calling? You should have seen the dashing young lover from next door who climbed over our fence. His name is Treasure. Oh, he has such a dear face . . .

Damn it all! What rubbish! Is she going to fill all of her letters with such stupid stuff? I want *people*, not dogs! I need **sustenance** to feed my soul. And all I get is this trash!

Let's skip a page. We may find something more interesting . . .

. . . Sophie was sitting at the table, sewing. I was looking out of the window. I like to watch the people who pass by.

Suddenly a servant came in and announced, "Teplov."

"Ask him in!" Sophie cried. She hugged me and murmured, "Oh Madgie, if you only knew who that is. He's

a Guards' officer. Such dark hair—and his eyes! Black as coals, and yet bright as fire."

Sophie rushed off to her room. A minute later a young officer with black side-whiskers entered. He went to the mirror and smoothed his hair. Then he glanced round the room. I growled a little and settled down by the window.

Soon Sophie came back and gave him a lively curtsey. I pretended to be busy looking out of the window. In fact, however, I cocked my head a little to overhear what they said.

Oh, you can't imagine, my dear, how silly their conversation was. They discussed some lady who danced the wrong step at a ball.

Then they talked about somebody called Bobov, who looked like a stork and nearly fell down. After that they mentioned a Lidina. This one thought she had blue eyes when they were really green, and so on.

How could you compare this officer to Treasure? Heavens, what a difference! First of all, the officer has a smooth, broad face. The only hair on his face is his side-whiskers. Those make him look as though he had a black kerchief tied round his face.

Treasure's face is thin, and he has a lovely white spot on his brow. His waist is much more slender than the officer's too. And his eyes and the way he carries himself are vastly different. You can't imagine how different!

I wonder what she sees in her officer. Why on earth is she so bewitched by him?

Yes, I too think something's strange about this. Something seems wrong. It is quite unbelievable that this officer should have swept her off her feet. Let's see.

If she's fallen for this officer, I think she'll soon be liking the clerk who sits in Papa's study. Oh, my dear, he's a real scarecrow. He looks just like a turtle caught in a bag . . .

Which clerk is this?

He has a peculiar name. All day long he sits and sharpens his quills. The hair on his head looks like straw. Papa sends him on errands instead of one of the servants . . .

The filthy mutt seems to be referring to me! What does she mean my hair is like straw?

Sophie can hardly keep from laughing when she sees him.

You damned, lying dog! What a filthy, **vile** tongue! As if I didn't know that jealousy is at the root of this!

I know whose tricks these are. It's the department chief who's responsible. That man has sworn undying hatred for me. He tries to hurt me at every turn.

Still, let's look at another letter. It may clear things up.

My dear Fidele,

Forgive me for not writing to you in such a long time. I've been in seventh heaven. I totally agree with the author who said that love is a second life.

Besides this, there have been a lot of changes in our house. The officer comes every day now. Sophie is madly in love with him. Papa is very merry.

I even heard our Gregory mumbling. (He always talks to himself while sweeping the floors.) He said that the wedding will be soon because Papa is determined to see Sophie married to a general, or high official, or a colonel . . .

Hell! I can't go on. High officials, senior officers—they always get all the best things. You find yourself a crumb of happiness and reach out for it. Then along comes a high official or an officer and snatches it away.

Damn! I'd like to become a general myself. Not that I want that just to obtain her hand in marriage.

No, I'd like to be a high official so I could watch them crawl around for my benefit. I'd listen for a while to their courtly jokes and then tell them just what I thought of them.

Oh hell, it hurts! I tore the stupid little dog's letter to bits.

DECEMBER 3

Impossible! Utter nonsense! There can't be a wedding. So what if he's in the Guards? That's nothing! It's just a kind of honor. You can't see it or touch it.

A Guards' officer doesn't have a third eye in the middle of his forehead. His nose isn't made of gold either. It's just the same as mine or anyone else's. He uses it to smell, not to eat. He sneezes with it, he doesn't cough.

I've often tried to discover the reason for all these differences. Why am I only a ninth-level clerk?[8] Why should I be a ninth-level clerk?

Perhaps I'm actually a general or a count and only seem to be a clerk? Maybe I don't really know who I am?

There are lots of examples in history. You'll hear of somebody quite common—not even a noble—some merchant or even a peasant who suddenly turns out to be a great lord or a baron. If it can happen to a peasant, what are the limits for a person of noble blood?

Suppose, for instance, I suddenly walked in wearing a general's uniform. There's an epaulet[9] on my right shoulder, an epaulet on my left. A blue sash across my chest.

How would that be? What tune would my lovely Sophie sing then?

And Papa, our director? What would he say?

Oh, he's really an ambitious one! He's a Mason,[10] no

---

[8]Government jobs were ranked by fourteen levels.

[9]An epaulet is a shoulder decoration on a uniform.

[10]A Mason is a member of a society that provides friendship and aid. The society is secret. Members recognize each other through special signs.

doubt about it, although he may pretend to be this or that. Right off I noticed that he only sticks out two fingers when he shakes hands.

But why can't I be promoted to general or governor or anything like that this moment? What I'd like to know is, why am I a clerk? Why precisely a clerk?

DECEMBER 5

I read the newspapers all morning. Strange things are happening in Spain. I can't even figure them out properly.

They write that the throne is now empty. The nobles are struggling to choose the successor. There's a lot of unrest in the country because of this.[11]

This seems very strange to me. How can a throne be empty? They say that some donna[12] may be the next monarch.

A donna cannot take the throne. It's totally impossible. A king should sit on the throne.

They say there is no king. But there must be a king! He must exist; he's just hidden away somewhere.

It's possible he's around but must hide for family reasons or for fear of some nearby country such as France. Or there may be other reasons.

DECEMBER 8

I was about to go to the office but various reasons held me back. I couldn't get this Spanish affair out of my head.

How can a donna become ruler? They won't allow it.

In the first place, England won't allow it. Then you must consider the policies of the rest of Europe: the Austrian

[11]After Ferdinand VII's death in 1833, there was a dispute over who would become the next ruler of Spain.

[12]Donna is a Spanish title for a woman.

Emperor, our Tsar . . . [13]

I confess I was so bothered and upset by these events that I couldn't do a lick of work all day. Marva remarked that I was very distracted during dinner.

In fact, I absent-mindedly threw two plates on the floor. Of course they broke at once.

After dinner, I walked the streets up and down. Did not observe anything of interest.

Then mostly lay on my bed and thought over the Spanish business.

YEAR 2000, APRIL 43

This is a day for great celebration. There is a new king of Spain. He has been discovered. *I* am the King.

I just discovered it today. To tell the truth, it all came to me in a flash.

I can't believe now that I could have imagined I was a mere clerk. How such **lunacy** ever entered my head is beyond me. It's lucky no one thought of putting me in a madhouse.

Now I see everything clearly. It all seems as plain as if it lay in the palm of my hand.

I can't understand it, but before, things seemed wrapped in a fog. I think the explanation for this is that people mistakenly believe the brain is located in the head. Of course it's not. The brain is carried in by winds from the Caspian Sea.

The first to whom I revealed my identity was Marva. When she heard that the King of Spain stood in front of her, she flung up her hands in awe. She nearly died of terror. The foolish woman had never seen a king of Spain before.

However, I tried to calm her. With some gracious words, I attempted to prove that I meant her well. I reassured her

---

[13]Tsar was once the term for a male ruler of Russia.

that I didn't hold a grudge for the sloppy job she sometimes did on my shoes.

The common folk are so ignorant. One can't talk to them of lofty things.

Doubtless she was so frightened because she thought that all kings of Spain are like Philip II.[14] But I carefully pointed out that Philip II and I were completely different.

Didn't go to the office. The hell with it! No, my friends, you won't lure me back there now. I'll never copy your dreadful documents again!

MARTOBER 86. BETWEEN DAY AND NIGHT

Today, one of the clerks came to my house to tell me to go to the office. He said I hadn't been there for over three weeks.

As a joke, I went. My department chief expected me to bow to him and apologize. But I just looked at him coolly—with not too much anger, nor a great deal of kindness either.

Then I sat down in my usual place, pretending to be **oblivious** to everyone else. I looked around at all that scribbling scum. I thought, if you only suspected who's sitting here among you. Oh Lord, what a fuss you'd make! The chief himself would give me a deep bow, just as he does for the director.

They put some papers in front of me. I was supposed to summarize them or something. I didn't lift a finger.

A few minutes later, a **commotion** occurred throughout the office. They said the director was on his way. Many clerks bumped into each other as they rushed forward. All of them hoped he'd notice them. But I didn't budge.

When the director passed through our department, everyone buttoned up their coats. I did nothing of the sort.

[14]Philip II (1527-1598) was a powerful king of Spain. He waged several wars to maintain and expand his huge empire. He also eliminated freedoms in nations he ruled in an effort to keep all power for himself.

So he's a director. What does that matter? He's really just an old cork, not a director at all. Yes, an ordinary cork, the kind used as a bottle stopper.

But the funniest thing of all was when they shoved a paper at me to sign. They thought I'd sign it in the very bottom corner, "Head Clerk such and such."

Well, let them think again! I wrote in the main space, the one the director uses, "Ferdinand VIII."

You should have seen the silence that followed. I merely waved my hand and said, "No need to demonstrate your devotion!" Then I walked out of the room.

From there, I went straight to the director's house. He was not at home. A servant tried to keep me out. But what I said made his arms drop limply to his sides.

I went straight to her bedroom. She was sitting in front of her mirror. She jumped up and stepped back when she saw me.

Still, I did not tell her that I was the King of Spain. I merely said that she couldn't even dream of the happiness awaiting her. I said that in spite of all our enemies' intrigues, we would be together.

I did not want to say more, so I left.

Oh, women are such crafty creatures! Only now do I see what they are like. So far, no one has found out who women love. I was the first to find out: Women love the devil. That's no joke!

Doctors write a lot of rubbish about women being this and that. But the fact is, they only love the devil.

Over there! You see that woman in the front **tier** of the boxes? The one raising her lorgnette?[15]

You think she's staring at that fat man with the star over there? Of course not. She's staring at the devil, who's hiding behind the fat man's back.

Now he's hidden himself in the star. He's beckoning to

[15]A lorgnette is a pair of glasses or small binoculars on a long handle.

her with his finger! And she'll marry him, no doubt about it.

As for all the rest—all those who lick boots and claim they're patriots—all they really want is money, money. Some patriots! They'd sell their mother, their father, and their God for money, those grubbing Judases!

All this crazy ambition is caused by a tiny bubble under the tongue. In that bubble is a small worm about the size of a pinhead.

And it's all the work of a barber who lives on Pea Street. I can't recall his name right now. But he and an old midwife[16] want to spread Islam all over the world. They say that in France most of the people have already become Moslems.

NO DATE. A DAY WITH NO DATE

Went along Nevsky Avenue **incognito**. Saw the Tsar drive past. Everyone was removing their hats, and so I did the same.

I gave no hint that I was the King of Spain. I thought it wouldn't be proper to reveal my identity there, before all those people. It would be more fitting if I appeared at court first.

What has prevented me from doing that is the fact that I haven't got Spanish royal dress. If I just could get hold of a cloak of some kind.

I wanted to have one made, but tailors are such idiots. Besides, they don't seem to take their trade seriously these days. They'd rather invest in shady deals. As a result, most of them end up mending roads.

I decided to have a cloak made out of my new uniform. I'd only worn it twice. But I didn't want those shiftless fools to botch it up. So I decided to do it myself.

---

[16]A midwife is a woman who assists in birthing babies.

I locked my door so no one would see me. I had to cut my uniform to pieces with the scissors. A cloak has a completely different style, you see.

DON'T REMEMBER THE DAY. NO MONTH EITHER. DAMNED IF I KNOW WHAT IT WAS.

The cloak is ready at last. Marva let out a holler when I put it on.

Yet I still don't feel ready to present myself at court. My retinue[17] hasn't yet arrived from Spain. It would be undignified to go without a retinue. I'm expecting them anytime.

DATE 1

I'm puzzled by how slow my retinue is. What can be holding them up? Maybe France? She's a most hostile nation.

I went to the post office and asked if the Spanish **delegates** had arrived.

But the postmaster is a total ass and knows nothing. "No," he says, "there are no Spanish delegates around here. But if you wish to send a letter, we'll accept it according to procedure."

Hell! What letter? Letters are garbage! Leave the letter writing to druggists . . .

MADRID, 30 FEBRUARIUS[18]

So I'm in Spain. It all happened so quickly that I hardly had time to know what occurred. This morning the Spanish

---

[17]A retinue is a group of people who accompany an important person.
[18]Madrid is the capital of Spain. Februarius is a combination of Spanish words for February and April.

delegates finally arrived for me. We all got into a carriage and drove off.

I was amazed by the speed we made. We went so fast that we reached the Spanish border in half an hour.

But then, there are now railroads all over Europe. The ships sail so fast too.

Spain is a strange country. In the first room we entered, I saw many people with shaven heads. I soon realized, though, that they must be either nobles or soldiers. In Spain, such people usually shave their heads.

The manners of the King's chancellor[19] also struck me as strange. He led me by the hand and then pushed me into a small room. He told me, "You sit there. And if you call yourself King Ferdinand again, I'll beat that nonsense out of your head."

But I knew that it was just a test, so I refused to give in. For this, the chancellor hit me twice across the back with a stick. The blows were so painful that I nearly cried out.

But I controlled myself. I remembered that this is normal custom among knights when they are given a high rank. To this day, they follow the rules of chivalry in Spain.

Left on my own, I decided to review some affairs of state. I discovered that China and Spain are actually one and the same land. It's only ignorance that leads people to call them separate countries.

Anyone who doubts this should just write the word "Spain" on a piece of paper. You'll see for yourself that it ends up as "China."

I also began to worry about a strange event that will take place tomorrow at seven. At that time, the earth will sit on the moon. The famous English chemist Wellington has predicted this.

I confess I was deeply troubled when I considered the moon's great delicacy and softness.

---

[19]A chancellor is the chief minister of state in some nations.

As is widely known, the moon is usually made in Hamburg. Really, they do a very shoddy job. I'm amazed England doesn't do something about it.

The moon is made by a lame cooper.[20] It's plain the fool has no idea what the moon should be like. He uses tarred rope and oil. That's why the Earth is filled with such a dreadful **stench** and you must hold your nose.

That's also the reason why the moon itself is such a delicate sphere. In fact, it's so delicate that humans can't live there—only noses.

This also explains why we can't see our own noses. They're all on the moon.

Then I thought about how heavy the earth is. It would grind our noses to a powder if it sat on the moon. I began to worry about this. I put on my socks and shoes. Then I rushed into the council room to order the police to prevent the earth from sitting on the moon.

The nobles with shaven heads—there were many in the council room—are very clever people. I said, "Gentlemen, let's save the moon. The earth is preparing to sit on it."

They all rushed at once to carry out my royal wish. Many tried to climb the wall to reach the moon. But at that moment, the chancellor appeared.

The instant they saw him, they scattered. Since I was King, I remained. But to my surprise, the chancellor hit me with his stick and drove me back into my room.

That just goes to show the power of popular custom in Spain!

JANUARY OF THE SAME YEAR, COMING AFTER FEBRUARIUS

I still don't understand what sort of a place Spain is. The customs and courtly manners are quite odd. I don't understand. I just don't understand any of it!

---

[20]A cooper makes wooden tubs and barrels.

Today, they shaved my head, though I shouted with all my strength that I didn't want to be a monk. I can scarcely even recall what happened after they began to drip cold water on my head. Never have I been through such hell! I was so distressed, they could hardly hold me down.

I just don't grasp the point of this strange custom. It seems so **inane**, so senseless! And the stupidity of the kings who never got around to doing away with this custom! It's quite beyond me.

After weighing all this, I've begun to think I must be in the hands of the Inquisition. The man I assumed was the chancellor must really be the Grand Inquisitor.[21]

But then, I can't see how a king can be at the mercy of the Inquisition. Of course, this could be the work of France and Polignac in particular.[22]

What a brute that Polignac is! He's sworn he'll be the death of me. And so he persecutes me.

But I know, my fine fellow, that the English are behind it all. The English are clever politicians. They've got a hand in every pot. The whole world knows that when England takes snuff, France sneezes.

DATE 25

Today the Grand Inquisitor entered my room. I heard his footsteps, so I hid under a chair.

He looked around. When he didn't see me, he began to call out. First it was "Aksentii Ivanov!" Then, "Clerk! Nobleman!"

Finally, "Ferdinand VIII, King of Spain!"

I almost stuck my head out. Then I thought to myself,

---

[21]The Inquisition was the religious watchdog of the Roman Catholic Church. This court arrested and tried unbelievers and enemies of the church. The Grand Inquisitor was chief of the court.

[22]Polignac (1780-1847) was a French statesman and foreign minister.

no, you won't trick me like that! I know that you just want to pour cold water on my head again.

But he spotted me and chased me out from under the chair with his stick. That damned stick hurts terribly.

I soon made a discovery that cheered me up. I had found that every rooster has his own Spain, tucked under his feathers.

The Grand Inquisitor left in a foul temper, threatening me with some punishment or other. Of course, I simply disregarded his helpless fury. I knew he was a puppet, a tool of the English.

DA 34 TE MTH. YRAE FEBRUARY 349

No, I can't bear it anymore. I haven't the strength.

My God! What are they doing to me? They pour cold water on my head. They won't listen to me or see me.

What have I done to them? Why are they torturing me this way? What do they want from a poor soul like me? What can I give them?

I have nothing to give. I don't even have any strength. I can't bear this torture. My head is on fire, and everything spins round me.

Save me! Take me away from here! Give me a troika[23] with horses swift as wind!

Come on, driver, let the harness bells ring! Soar upward, my horses, carry me away from this world! Further, further, to where nothing can be seen, nothing!

The sky whirls around me. A star gleams far away. The forest rushes past with its dark trees and the crescent moon. A violet fog stretches out like a carpet below. The twanging of a guitar string pierces the fog.

---

[23]A troika is a carriage pulled by three horses.

On one side is the sea; on the other is Italy. Now the Russian huts come into view.

Is that my house over there, looming blue in the distance? And is that my mother sitting by the window?

Mother, save your wretched son! Drop your tears on his throbbing head! See how they torture him! Hold this poor orphan in your arms. There's no room for him in this world. They persecute him. Mother, have pity on your sick child . . .

By the way, did you know that the Bey of Algiers[24] has a wart right under his nose?

---

[24]Bey is a Mideastern title for a governor.

"The Diary of a Madman" was first published in 1835.

INSIGHTS INTO
NIKOLAI GOGOL

(1809-1852)

Gogol was born in Sorochintsy, Russia.

Gogol has often been called one of Russia's greatest authors. Yet in school he ranked as a below-average student. His teachers called him lazy. Fellow students called him "the mysterious dwarf." Gogol's pale and ugly features, skinny build, and wild mood swings earned him the title.

Once in a fit of enthusiasm, Gogol roped his schoolmates into putting on a play. His superb talent as director, actor, and clown thrilled the class.

Gogol could play serious roles too. Once he was caught playing a dirty trick at school. To avoid being punished, Gogol acted as though he were insane. He played his part so well that instead of being punished, he was ordered to rest quietly for a few weeks. Gogol took advantage of the time to read and write.

Early in his life, Gogol knew he was destined to be great. The problem was, he was not sure *how* he would become great.

When Gogol left school in 1828, he took a job in the government. He soon found the work boring. He realized he must seek greatness elsewhere.

Next Gogol decided he would be a great poet. He wrote a long poem but failed to find anyone who would publish it. So Gogol published the poem at his own expense.

Unfortunately, the poem was bad and critics bluntly put it down. Gogol and a servant rushed out to buy all the remaining copies of the poem and destroy them.

Other career attempts followed. Gogol taught history at a young women's school and later at a university.

Then, in 1836, Gogol's break came. That year his comedy *The Inspector General* was staged. Some praised it wildly; others scorned it. But admirer or critic, everyone was talking about Gogol. At last Gogol had found his path to greatness.

Gogol believed he had a mission to serve his country. With this aim in mind, Gogol turned his writing into a tool for social reform.

Gogol saw and disliked the upper class's scornful attitude toward the poor. He expressed his views in his tale "The Overcoat." The message of the story was clear to all: The poor should be treated as people of value.

Other works by Gogol:
"The Carriage," short story
"Nevsky Avenue," short story
"The Nose," short story
Dead Souls, novel

THE NECKLACE

GUY DE MAUPASSANT

VOCABULARY PREVIEW

Below is a list of words that appear in the story. Read the list and get to know the words before you start the story.

adulation—great flattery or praise
aghast—anxious and fearful
chagrin—irritation, shame, or disappointment
distinguished—famous; notable
drawn—looking strained and careworn
economical—thrifty; not wasteful
elated—overjoyed
exorbitant—outrageously high or great (usually said of a price)
haggled—argued about the terms of a deal; bargained
hailing—calling or signaling
imploring—pleading
jeopardy—danger; risk
luxuries—costly, pleasurable things that are not absolutely necessary
modest—plain and inexpensive
naive—innocent and simple
poverty—poorness
predicament—a difficult or puzzling situation
prospect—outlook
scouring—scrubbing
vexation—annoyance; irritation

MT. LOGAN MIDDLE SCHOOL
MEDIA CENTER

The Necklace

· ·

GUY de MAUPASSANT

Can a diamond necklace transform the wife of a lowly clerk into Cinderella? Maybe so, for with such a necklace, Mathilde's night at the ball is a dream come true.

Yet the magic evening does end. And then Mathilde and her husband waken to learn the cost of the dream.

She was one of those pretty, charming young ladies, born into a family of clerks as if by mistake. She had no dowry,[1] no hopes. Nor did she have any means of meeting and marrying a rich and **distinguished** man. So she finally married a minor clerk in the Ministry of Education.

Her tastes were simple because she had never been able to buy rich clothes. But she was unhappy, like one who was not in her proper class.

[1] A dowry is a gift of money or property given to the groom by the bride's family at the time of marriage.

You see, women do not belong to any fixed class or rank. Their grace, beauty, and charm serve them in place of noble birth and family. These traits are their claim to nobility. Some daughters of common people are so gifted that they become equal to great ladies.

She suffered continually, feeling herself born for delicate things and **luxuries**. She suffered from the **poverty** of her apartment. The shabby walls, the worn chairs, and the faded drapes caused her pain. Another woman in her position might not have noticed all these things. But they tortured and angered her.

The sight of the little Breton[2] maid who did the housework awoke sad regrets and desperate dreams in her. She dreamt of quiet chambers with Oriental hangings. In her imagination, tall bronze lamps lighted those rooms. Two huge butlers in short trousers—drowsy from the heavy air from the heater—slept in the large armchairs.

She dreamt of large halls. In those rooms, she imagined old silk hangings and graceful furniture with valuable knickknacks.

She dreamt of small, perfumed, charming apartments. Such rooms were made for five o'clock chats with very close friends. These friends would be distinguished, popular men whose company every woman desired.

When she sat down to dinner at the round table, the dreams continued. In reality, the same cloth had been on the table for three days. Her husband, who sat across from her, uncovered the serving bowl with a delighted air. "Oh, a good potpie! I know nothing better than that—" he said.

But she dreamt of elegant dinners and gleaming silverware. She pictured wall hangings that filled the room with ancient people and strange birds in the midst of fairy forests.

She dreamt of wonderful food served in marvelous dishes. Whispered compliments, which she would listen to with the

[2]A Breton is a person from Brittany, a northwestern section of France.

smile of a sphinx,[3] came to her ear. And all the while, she would be eating rosy trout or a pheasant's wing.

She had neither party dresses nor jewels—nothing. And she longed for just those things. She felt that she was made for them. She had such a desire to please, to be envied, to be clever and courted.

She had a rich friend—a classmate from her schooldays at the convent—whom she did not like to visit. She suffered so much when she returned home from one of those visits. And she wept for whole days from **chagrin**, regret, despair, and anguish.

One evening, her husband returned home **elated**. He proudly carried in his hand a large envelope.

"Look," he said. "Here is something for you."

She quickly tore open the envelope. Then she drew out a printed card on which there were these words.

> The Minister of Education and Madame George Ramponneau ask the honor of Monsieur and Madame[4] Loisel's company. Please come Monday evening, January 18, to the Minister's home.

Her husband had hoped that she would be delighted. But, instead, she threw the invitation spitefully down upon the table. She murmured, "What do you suppose I want with that?"

"But, my dear, I thought it would make you happy. You never get a chance to go out. And this is a fine occasion! I had a great deal of trouble to get an invitation. Everybody wants one, and it is much sought after. Not many are given to clerks. You'll see the most distinguished people there."

She looked at him with an irritated eye. "What do you think I have to wear to such a thing?"

[3]The sphinx is a mythical creature with a lion's body and a human face.
[4]Monsieur and Madame are French for Mr. and Mrs.

He had not thought of that. He stammered, "Why, the dress you wear when we go to the theater. It seems very pretty to me—"

He fell silent, stunned and dismayed to see his wife burst out weeping. Two great tears fell slowly from the corners of her eyes toward the corners of her mouth. He stammered, "What's the matter? What's the matter?"

By a violent effort, she controlled her **vexation**. Wiping her wet cheeks, she responded in a calm way.

"Nothing. Only I don't have a dress, and, therefore, can't go to this affair. Give your card to some co-worker whose wife has a better wardrobe than I."

He was upset but answered, "Let's see, Mathilde. How much would a suitable costume cost? Something that you could wear for other occasions? Something very simple?"

She reflected for some seconds, making estimates. She was trying to think of a sum she could ask for without being immediately refused. She did not wish to frighten the **economical** clerk.

Finally she said, "I can't tell exactly. But it seems to me that four hundred francs[5] should cover it."

He turned a little pale. He has saved just this sum to buy a rifle. He wanted to join some hunting parties the next summer with friends who shot larks near Nanterre.[6]

Nonetheless, he answered, "Very well. I'll give you four hundred francs. But try to get a pretty dress."

The day of the ball approached. Madame Loisel seemed sad, disturbed, and anxious. Yet her dress was nearly ready.

Her husband said to her one evening, "What's the matter with you? You have acted strangely for two or three days."

[5]A franc is a piece of French money. At the time of the story, the sum was equal to about $80.
[6]Nanterre is a town near Paris.

And she responded, "I am annoyed not to have a jewel—not one gem—nothing to adorn myself with. I shall look so poor. I'd almost prefer not to go to this party."

He replied, "You can wear some flowers. This season, they're very fashionable. For ten francs you can have two or three magnificent roses."

She was not convinced. "No," she replied. "There's nothing more humiliating than to look shabby in the midst of rich women."

Then her husband cried out, "How stupid we are! Go see your friend Madame Forestier. Ask her to lend you her jewels. You know her well enough to do that."

She cried out in joy. "It's true!" she said. "I hadn't thought of that."

The next day she went to her friend's house and told about her **predicament**.

Madame Forestier went to her closet with the mirror doors. There she took out a large jewel case. Bringing it back, she opened it and said, "Choose, my dear."

She saw at first some bracelets, then a pearl necklace. Next she noticed a cross of gold and jewels from Venice. The workmanship was wonderful.

She tried on the jewels before the mirror. Still she hesitated. She was not able to decide which to take and which to leave.

Then she asked, "Have you nothing more?"

"Why, yes. Look for yourself. I don't know what will please you."

Suddenly she discovered, in a black satin box, a superb necklace of diamonds. Her heart beat fast with intense longing. Her hands trembled as she grasped the necklace. She placed the jewels about her throat against her dress and stared at them in ecstasy.

Then she asked in an **imploring** voice, "Could you lend me this? Just this and nothing more?"

"Why, yes, of course."

She opened her arms and embraced her friend with passion. Then she fled with her treasure.

The day of the ball arrived. Madame Loisel was a great success. She was the prettiest of all—elegant, gracious, smiling, and full of joy.

All the men noticed her, asked her name, and begged to be introduced. All the members of the Cabinet wished to waltz with her. The Minister himself paid her some attention.

She danced with enthusiasm and passion. She was drunk with pleasure. The triumph of her beauty and the glory of success filled her. She was floating on a cloud of happiness. She was thrilled by all this **adulation**, this admiration, and these awakened desires. This victory, so complete and sweet to the heart of a woman, enwrapped her.

She went home about four o'clock in the morning. Since midnight, her husband had been half asleep in one of the little side rooms. Three other gentlemen whose wives were also enjoying themselves were there, too.

He threw around her shoulders the wraps they had carried for coming home. These were **modest** garments of everyday wear. Their poorness clashed with the elegance of her ball costume.

She felt this and wished to hurry away. She did not want to be noticed by the other women who were wrapping themselves in rich furs.

Loisel held her back. "Wait," he said. "You'll catch cold out there. I'll call a cab."

But she would not listen and went down the steps rapidly. When they were in the street, they found no carriage. They set out to find one, **hailing** the coachmen whom they saw in the distance.

They walked along toward the Seine,[7] hopeless and shivering. Finally they found on the dock one of those old

[7]The Seine is a river that flows through Paris.

carriages that one sees in Paris after nightfall. It seems as if they are too ashamed of their shabbiness to come out in the daytime.

The carriage took them as far as their door on Martyr Street. They went wearily up to their apartment. For her, it was all over. And for his part, he remembered that he would have to be at the office by ten o'clock.

She removed the wraps from her shoulders before the mirror. She wanted a final view of herself in all her glory.

Suddenly she cried out. Her necklace was gone.

Her husband, already half undressed, asked, "What's the matter?"

She turned toward him excitedly. "I have—I have—I don't have Madame Forestier's necklace."

He arose in dismay. "What! How can that be! It's not possible!"

And they looked in the folds of the dress, in the folds of the cloak, in the pockets—everywhere. They could not find it.

He asked, "Are you sure you still had it when we left the ball?"

"Yes, I felt it in the entryway as we came out."

"But if you lost it in the street, we'd have heard it fall. It must be in the cab."

"Yes. It's likely. Did you get its number?"

"No. And you, did you notice it?"

"No."

They looked at each other **aghast**. Finally Loisel dressed himself again.

He said, "I am going over our route to see if I can find it."

And he went. She remained in her evening gown, not even having the energy to go to bed. She remained stretched upon a chair, without ambition or thoughts.

Toward seven o'clock her husband returned. He had found nothing.

He went to the police and to the cab offices. He put an

ad in the newspapers offering a reward. He did everything that offered them the slightest bit of hope.

She waited all day in a state of bewilderment. Loisel returned that evening, his face pale and **drawn**. He had discovered nothing.

"It will be necessary," he said, "to write to your friend. Say that you have broken the clasp of her necklace and that you are having it repaired. That will give us time to think."

She wrote as he dictated.

At the end of a week, they had lost all hope. And Loisel— now looking five years older—declared, "We must take measures to replace the necklace."

The next day they took the box the necklace had come in to the jeweler whose name was on the inside. He checked his records.

"It is not I, Madame, who sold this necklace," he said. "I only provided the box."

They went from jeweler to jeweler seeking a necklace like the other one, searching their memories. Both of them were sick with chagrin and anxiety.

In a shop of the Palias Royal,[8] they found a diamond necklace which seemed to them exactly like the lost one. It was valued at forty thousand francs. They could get it for thirty-six thousand.

They begged the jeweler not to sell it for three days. And they arranged so that they might return it for thirty-four thousand if they found the other one by the end of February.

Loisel had eighteen thousand francs which his father had left him. He borrowed the rest.

He borrowed by asking for a thousand francs from one, five hundred from another, a hundred from this one, sixty from that. He signed IOUs and made promises that would

---

[8]The Palias Royal is a section of Paris with expensive shops.

ruin him. He took money from loan sharks and all kinds of moneylenders.

In fact, he put his entire existence in **jeopardy**. He dared to sign IOUs without even knowing whether he could repay them or not.

Tortured by anxiety, by black misery, and by the **prospect** of all the sacrifices and torments of his conscience that lay ahead, he went to get the new necklace. On the merchant's counter, he deposited thirty-six thousand francs.

When Madame Loisel took back the necklace to Madame Forestier, her friend said in an icy tone, "You should have returned it to me sooner. I might have needed it."

She didn't open the jewel box as Madame Loisel feared she would. If she had noticed the substitution, what would she have thought? What would she have said? Would Madame Forestier have taken her for a robber?

Madame Loisel now knew the horrible life of great poverty. She did her part, however, with newfound heroism. It was necessary to pay this frightful debt. She would pay it.

They sent away the maid. They moved to another building and rented some attic rooms.

She learned the heavy household chores, the disgusting work of a kitchen. She cleaned dishes, **scouring** the greasy pots and pans with her rosy nails. She washed the dirty linen, the shirts and dishclothes, which she hung on a line to dry.

She took the trash down to the street each morning. Then she brought up the water, stopping at each landing to catch her breath.

And, clothed like a common woman, she went to the grocer's, the butcher's, and the fruit seller's. With her basket on her arm, she shopped. She **haggled** with the merchants down to the last penny.

Every month, it was necessary to renew some IOUs—to get more time—and to pay others.

The husband worked evenings, putting the account books

of some merchant in order. At nights he often did copying for five pennies a page.

And this went on for ten years.

At the end of ten years, they had repaid everything. Everything, including the **exorbitant** interest of the moneylender and the compound interest, too.[9]

Madame Loisel looked old now. She had become a stout, loud woman—the crude woman of a poor household. Her hair was uncombed, her skirts were twisted, her hands red. She spoke in a harsh tone and scrubbed the floors with large pails of water.

But sometimes, when her husband was at the office, she would sit before the window and think of that evening party long ago. Again she would recall that ball where she was so beautiful and so flattered.

How would it have been if she had not lost that necklace? Who knows? Who can tell? How strange life is! How full of changes! How little a thing will ruin or save you!

One Sunday she took a walk on the Champs-Elysees[10] to forget her worries. As she strolled, she suddenly noticed a woman walking with a child. It was Madame Forestier—still looking young, pretty, and attractive.

Madame Loisel felt a flood of emotion. Should she speak to her? Yes, certainly. And now that she had paid, she would tell her everything. Why not?

Madame Loisel approached her. "Good day, Jeanne."

Her friend did not recognize her. In fact, she was astonished to be addressed in such a familiar way by this common person.

She stammered, "But, Madame—I do not know—You must be mistaken."

[9]Compound interest is the amount paid on both the original sum and interest added to that sum.

[10]Champs-Elysees is the major avenue in Paris.

"No, I am Mathilde Loisel."

Her friend cried out in astonishment. "Oh, my poor Mathilde! How you've changed—"

"Yes, I've had some hard times since I last saw you. Some miserable days, too—and all on account of you."

"Because of me? What do you mean?"

"You remember the diamond necklace that you loaned me to go to the ball at the Ministry?"

"Yes, very well."

"Well, I lost it."

"How can that be! You returned it."

"I returned another to you exactly like it. And we have paid for it over the past ten years. You can guess that it wasn't easy for us when we had nothing. But it's over and I am content."

Madame Forestier stopped short. She said, "You say that you bought a diamond necklace to replace mine?"

"Yes. You never noticed the difference, then? They were just alike."

And she smiled with a proud and **naive** joy.

Madame Forestier was deeply touched and took both Madame Loisel's hands in her own. "Oh, my poor Mathilde! Mine were not real. They were worth at most five hundred francs!"

"The Necklace" was first published in 1884.

INSIGHTS INTO
GUY DE MAUPASSANT

(1850-1893)

Maupassant was born in Normandy, France.

Maupassant is considered a master of the short story. In fact, his lean, tight writing style actually helped shape the form of the short story.

Maupassant's talent in writing tales was quickly revealed. As a beginning writer, he joined a group of authors that included the novelist Emile Zola. This group decided to publish a collection of anti-war stories.

Maupassant's contribution was his second published story, "Ball of Fat." It instantly made a name for him and set him above the rest of the young writers.

Before Maupassant's success as a writer, he worked as a government clerk. He hated this job and lived only for the weekends.

Saturdays he spent boating and drinking with friends. He was even known to try and impress the ladies with his great skill as an oarsman.

On Sundays a more serious side of the man was revealed. On that day he visited his advisor, the great writer Gustave Flaubert. Maupassant would listen and absorb all he could from the master's criticism of his work.

Maupassant was one of the most productive writers of all time. From 1880 until 1990 he wrote 300 short stories, six novels, and 200 articles and essays.

At an early age, Maupassant contracted syphilis. His headaches from this disease were so severe that he could not read or write for days. He sought relief by taking drugs and traveling on his boat (named after his novel *Bel Ami*). But nothing helped. The disease only grew worse.

The agony of this disease even crept into Maupassant's work. His short story "Lo Honla" was written while the author was racked by hallucinations. As a result, the tale curiously resembles the work of Edgar Allan Poe.

Other works by Maupassant:
  "Ball of Fat," short story
  "Miss Harriet," short story
  "Moonlight," short story
  "A Piece of String," short story
  A Life, book
  The Two Brothers, book

THE BISHOP'S CANDLESTICKS
VICTOR HUGO

VOCABULARY PREVIEW

Below is a list of words that appear in the story. Read the list and get to know the words before you start the story.

asylum—shelter; place of safety
attentive—alert and observant
comprehended—understood; grasped
contemplates—considers or examines
deposited—placed or put down
despise—scorn and look down upon
furtive—secret and sly
hospitable—entertaining guests with friendliness and courtesy
humane—kindhearted and sympathetic; ready to help others
ignominy—disgrace; shame
inarticulate—unspoken or spoken unclearly
intermittent—occurring once in a while; periodic
interval—pause or space between two things
liberated—freed
luminous—glowing from within; sending out light
novel—new or unusual
repose—rest
sublime—grand and glorious
tumult—uproar; great unrest
voracity—extreme greediness

The Bishop's Candlesticks

After nineteen years as a prisoner, criminal Jean Valjean has finally been freed. But freedom does not erase his past. Turned away by many, Jean finally stumbles into the Bishop's household. There he finds a saintly welcome—as well as a devilish temptation.

There was a rather loud knock at the front door.

"Come in," said the Bishop.

The door was thrown wide open, as if someone were pushing it with great energy and determination. A man entered and stopped, leaving the door open behind him. He had his knapsack on his shoulder and his stick in his hand. In his eyes was a rough, bold, wearied, and violent expression. The firelight fell on him; he was hideous. He looked evil.

The Bishop fixed a quiet eye on the man and opened his mouth. Undoubtedly he intended to ask the newcomer what he wanted.

Victor Hugo

The man leaned both his hands on his stick and looked in turn at the two aged women and the old man. Not waiting for the Bishop to speak, he said in a loud voice, "My name is Jean Valjean. I am a galley slave[1] and have spent nineteen years as a prisoner.

"I was **liberated** four days ago and started for Pontarlier, which is where I want to go. I have been walking four days since I left Toulon. Today I have walked nearly thirty-five miles.

"This evening on coming into town I went to the inn. But I was sent away because of my yellow passport, which I had shown at the police office.

"I went to another inn. There the landlord said to me, 'Be off!' It was the same everywhere. No one would have anything to do with me.

"I went to the prison, but the jailer would not take me in. I got into a dog's kennel. But the dog bit me and drove me off as if it had been a man. It seemed to know who I was.

"I went into the fields to sleep in the starlight, but there were no stars. I thought it would rain. And since there was no God to prevent it from raining, I came back to the town to sleep in a doorway.

"I was lying down on a stone in the square when a good woman pointed to your house. She told me, 'Go and knock there.'

"What sort of a house is this? Do you run an inn? I have money—109 francs and 15 sous[2]—which I earned by my nineteen years' toil. I will pay. After all, what do I care about that since I have money!

"I am very tired and frightfully hungry. Will you let me stay here?"

---

[1]The French sentenced some criminals to be galley slaves. These men were forced to row ships (galleys).

[2]Francs and sous are French coins.

"Madame[3] Magloire," said the Bishop, "you will put on another knife and fork."

The man advanced three paces and approached the lamp which was on the table.

"Wait a minute," he continued, as if he had not **comprehended**, "that will not do. Did you not hear me say that I was a galley slave—a convict—and have just come from prison?"

He took from his pocket a large yellow paper, which he unfolded. "Here is my passport—yellow as you see—which gets me kicked out wherever I go. Will you read it? I can read it. I learned to read at the prison. There is a prison school for those who want to attend it.

"This is what is written in my passport: 'Jean Valjean, a liberated convict. Born in—but that does not concern you. Has served in the galleys for nineteen years. Five years for robbery with housebreaking. Fourteen years for having tried to escape four times. The man is very dangerous.'

"All the world has turned me away. So are you willing to receive me? Is this an inn? Will you give me some food and a bed? Have you a stable?"

"Madame Magloire," said the Bishop, "you will put clean sheets on the bed in the alcove."[4]

Then he turned to Jean. "Sit down and warm yourself, sir. We shall eat soon. Your bed will be made ready while we are eating."

The man understood this at once. The expression of his face had been gloomy and harsh to this moment. Now it was marked with surprise, joy, and doubt. He began stammering like a madman.

"Is it true? You will let me stay? You will not turn me out, a convict?

---

[3]Madame is French for Mrs. Mademoiselle (abbreviated Mlle.) means Miss and Monsieur means Mr.

[4]An alcove is a recessed or hollowed out part of a room.

"You call me 'sir,' you do not humiliate me. 'Get out, dog!' That is what is always said to me. I really believed you would turn me out. That's why I told you at once who I am!

"Oh, what a worthy woman she was who sent me here! I shall have supper and a bed with mattresses and sheets, like everyone else. For nineteen years I have not slept in a bed!

"You really mean that I am to stay! You are worthy people. Besides, I have money and will pay very well.

"By the way, what is your name, landlord? I will pay anything you please, for you are a worthy man. You keep an inn, do you not?"

"I am," said the Bishop, "a priest, living in this house."

"A priest?" the man continued. "Oh! what a worthy priest! I suppose you will not ask me for money. The curé,[5] I suppose, the cure of that big church? Oh, yes, what a fool I am. I did not notice your robe."

While speaking, he **deposited** his knapsack and stick in a corner. Then he returned his passport to his pocket and sat down.

"You are **humane**, sir, and do not feel contempt. A good priest is very good. Then you do not want me to pay?"

"No," said the Bishop, "keep your money. How long did you take to earn your 100 francs?"

"Nineteen years."

"Nineteen years!" The Bishop gave a deep sigh.

The man went on. "I still have all my money. In four days I have spent only 25 sous, which I earned by helping to unload carts at Grasse.

"Since you are an abbé,[6] I will tell you. We had a chaplain at the galleys. One day I saw a bishop, a Monseigneur as they call him. He is the curé over the curés.

[5]A curé is a French priest of a parish (lower in rank than a bishop).
[6]An abbé is a French title for a priest.

"But pardon me, you must know that in your situation. We convicts know and explain such things badly. For me in particular it is so far away in the past.

"This bishop said mass in the middle of the prison at an altar. He had a pointed gold thing on his head. It glistened in the bright sunshine.

"We were lined up on three sides of a square, with guns and lighted matches facing us. He spoke, but was too far off, and we did not hear him. That is what a bishop is."

While the man was speaking, the Bishop had gone to close the door, which had been left open. Madame Magloire came in. She brought a silver spoon and fork, which she placed on the table.

"Madame Magloire," said the Bishop, "set his place as near as you can to the fire." Turning to his guest, he said, "The night breeze is sharp on the Alps. You must be cold, sir."

Each time he said the word "sir" with his gentle, grave voice, the man's face brightened. "Sir" to a convict is the glass of water to the shipwrecked sailor of the *Medusa*.[7] **Ignominy** thirsts for respect.

"This lamp gives a very bad light," the Bishop continued. Madame Magloire understood. She fetched from the chimney of Monseigneur's bedroom the two silver candlesticks, which she placed on the table already lighted.

"Monsieur le Curé," said the man, "you are good and do not **despise** me. Yet I have not hidden where I came from, nor that I am an unfortunate fellow."

The Bishop, who was seated by his side, gently touched his hand. "You need not have told me who you were. This is not my house but the house of Christ. This door does not ask a man who enters whether he has a name, only if he has sorrow.

---

[7]*The Raft of the Medusa* is a painting by French artist Thedore Gericault (1791-1824). It shows a group of shipwrecked sailors clinging to a raft.

"You are suffering; you are hungry and thirsty. So be welcome. And do not thank me or say that I am receiving you in my house. No one is at home here except the man who has need of an **asylum**.

"I tell you, who are a passerby, that you are more at home here than I am myself. Everything here is yours.

"Why should I want to know your name? Besides, before you told it to me, you had one which I knew."

The man opened his eyes in amazement.

"Is that true? You know my name?"

"Yes," the Bishop answered, "you are my brother."

"Monsieur le Curé," the man exclaimed, "I was very hungry when I came in. But you are so kind that I do not know at present what I feel. It has passed."

The Bishop looked at him and said, "You have suffered greatly?"

"Oh! the red jacket,[8] the ball and chain on your foot, a plank to sleep on. Heat, cold, labor; the gang of men, the beatings. The double chain for nothing at all. A dungeon for a word—even when you are ill in bed. And the chain gang. Even the dogs are happier.

"Nineteen years, and now I am forty-six. And, at present, the yellow passport!"

"Yes," said the Bishop, "you have come from a place of sorrow. Listen to me. There will be more joy in Heaven when a sinner tearfully repents than when a hundred good men receive their white robes.

"If you leave that mournful place with thoughts of hatred and anger against your fellow men, you are worthy of pity. If you leave it with thoughts of kindness, gentleness, and peace, you are worth more than any of us."

In the meanwhile Madame Magloire had served the soup. It was made of water, oil, bread, salt, and a little bacon.

---

[8]The red jacket was a French uniform for galley slaves.

The rest of the supper consisted of a piece of mutton, figs, fresh cheese, and a loaf of rye bread. She had herself added a bottle of old wine.

The Bishop's face suddenly assumed the expression of gaiety that **hospitable** natures often show. "Let us eat," he said eagerly, as was his custom when any stranger supped with him.

He asked the man sit to down on his right. Meanwhile Mlle. Baptistine, his sister, took her seat on his left. She was perfectly peaceful and natural.

The Bishop said grace. Then he served the soup himself, as was his custom. The man began eating greedily.

All at once the Bishop said, "It strikes me that there is something missing on the table."

To tell the truth, Madame Magloire had only put out the absolutely necessary silver. Now it was the custom in this house when the Bishop had anyone to supper to arrange the whole set of silverware on the table.

The silverware served as an innocent display. The graceful appearance of luxury was a kind of childishness full of charm in this strict and gentle house which raised poorness to dignity.

Madame Magloire took the hint and went out without a word. A moment later, the remaining spoons and forks glittered on the cloth, neatly arranged before each guest.

The man paid no attention to anyone. He ate with frightful **voracity**.

But after supper he said, "Monsieur le Curé, all this is much too good for me. Yet I am bound to say that the cart drivers who would not let me sup with them have better food than you."

"They have to work harder than I do."

"No," the man continued, "they have more money. You are poor, as I can plainly see. Perhaps you are not even a curé. Ah, if Heaven were just, you ought to be a curé."

"Heaven is more than just," said the Bishop.

After bidding his sister good night, the Bishop picked up one of the silver candlesticks. Handing the other to his guest, he said, "I will lead you to your room, sir."

The man followed him. In order to reach the little chapel where the alcove was, they had to pass through the Bishop's bedroom. At the moment they went through the room, Madame Magloire was putting away the silverware in the cupboard over the bed. It was the last thing she did every night before going to bed.

The Bishop led his guest to the alcove. There a clean bed had been prepared for him. The man placed the branched candlestick on a small table.

"I trust you will have a good night," said the Bishop.

As two o'clock rang from the cathedral bell, Jean Valjean awoke. What roused him was that the bed was too comfortable. For close to twenty years he had not slept in a bed.

Though he had not undressed, the sensation was too **novel** not to disturb his sleep. He had been asleep for more than four hours and his weariness had worn off. He opened his eyes and looked into the surrounding darkness. Then he closed them again to go to sleep once more.

When three o'clock struck, he opened his eyes and suddenly sat up. He stretched out his arms and felt for his knapsack, which he had thrown into a corner. Then he let his legs hang and felt himself seated on the bed almost without knowing how.

He remained for a while thinking in this position. It would have seemed a little sinister if anyone had seen him, the only person awake in the house. All at once he stooped and took off his shoes. Then he again fell into his thoughtful posture and remained motionless.

To work! He rose, hesitated for a moment, and listened. All was silent in the house. He went on tiptoe to the window, through which he peered.

The night was not very dark. The wind chased heavy clouds across the face of the full moon. This produced lights and shadows and a kind of twilight in the room. The twilight was enough to light Jean Valjean's way but **intermittent** because of the clouds. It resembled that black and blue hue produced by a cellar grate over which people continually pass.

Jean Valjean reached the window which looked out onto the garden. He examined it. There were no bars on it. It was only closed, as was usual in the country, by a small peg.

He opened the window. But a cold, sharp breeze suddenly entered the room, so he immediately closed it. He gazed into the garden with that **attentive** glance which studies rather than looks. He found that the yard was enclosed by a whitewashed wall, easy to climb over. Beyond it he noticed the tops of trees standing at regular distances. This proved that the wall separated the garden from a public street.

After taking this glance, he walked boldly to the alcove. There he opened his knapsack and took out something which he laid on the bed. He then put his shoes in one of the pouches, placed the knapsack on his shoulders, and put on his cap. After pulling the peak down over his eyes, he reached for his stick. He placed that on the window.

Finally he returned to the bed and took up the object he had laid on it. It resembled a short iron bar, sharpened at one end. It would have been difficult to tell in the dark for what purpose this piece of iron had been fashioned. Perhaps it was a lever, perhaps it was a club.

By daylight it could have been seen that it was nothing but a miner's candlestick. The convicts of that day were sometimes employed in getting rock from the lofty hills that surround Toulon. It was not unusual for them to have mining tools to work with. Miners' candlesticks are made of heavy steel and have a point at the lower end, by which they are dug into the rock.

He took the bar in his right hand. Holding his breath and deadening his footsteps, he walked toward the door of the next room. This was the Bishop's bedroom, as we know.

On reaching this door he found it open. The Bishop had not shut it.

Jean Valjean listened, but there was not a sound. He pushed the door lightly with the tip of his finger. He pushed with the **furtive**, restless gentleness of a cat that wants to get in. The door yielded to the pressure. It made an almost unnoticeable and silent movement, which slightly widened the opening.

He waited for a moment. Then he pushed the door again more boldly.

The first danger had passed. Still there was a fearful **tumult** within him. Yet he did not step back. He had not done so even when he thought himself lost. He only thought of finishing the job as speedily as possible. He entered the bedroom.

The room was in a state of perfect calmness. Here and there might be seen confused and vague forms. By day these forms were papers scattered over the table, open volumes, books piled on a sofa, an easychair covered with clothes, and a prayer desk. But at this moment, all were only dark corners and patches of white.

Jean Valjean advanced cautiously and carefully, avoiding the furniture. He heard from the end of the room the calm and regular breathing of the sleeping Bishop.

Suddenly he stopped, for he was close to the bed. He had reached it sooner than he thought he would.

Nature at times blends her effect and appearance with our actions with a gloomy and intelligent design. It is as though she wishes to make us stop and think.

For nearly half an hour, a heavy cloud had covered the sky. But at the moment when Jean Valjean stopped at the foot of the bed, this cloud was torn apart as if on purpose.

A moonbeam passing through the tall window suddenly lit up the Bishop's pale face. He was sleeping peacefully and was wrapped in a long garment of brown wool, which covered his arms down to the wrists. His head was thrown back on the pillow in the easy attitude of **repose**. His hand, with the ring of his office, and which had done so many good deeds, hung out of bed.

His entire face was lit up by a vague expression of satisfaction, hope, and blessedness. It was more than a smile— almost a glorious beam. On his forehead was a holy reflection of an invisible light. While asleep, the soul of a just man **contemplates** a mysterious heaven.

A reflection of this heaven was cast over the Bishop. But it was at the same time a **luminous** glow, for the heaven was inside him. This heaven was his conscience.

At the moment when the moonbeam was cast over this internal light, the sleeping Bishop seemed to be surrounded by a glory. But this glory was veiled by a strange half light.

The moon, the slumbering landscape, the quiet house, the hour, the silence, the moment. All of this added something solemn to the bishop's repose, something hard to describe. The scene cast a majestic, calm halo round his white hair and closed eyes. The halo framed his face—which was all hope and confidence—his aged head, and his childlike slumber.

There was almost a godlike element in this unconsciously great man.

Jean Valjean was standing in the shadow with his crowbar in his hand, motionless and terrified by this luminous old man. He had never seen anything like this before. Such confidence horrified him.

The moral world has no greater sight than this: a troubled, restless conscience, about to commit a sin, watching the sleep of a just man.

The sleep of this man, so alone while Jean Valjean stood over him, had something **sublime** about it. And the convict felt this vaguely but commandingly.

No one could have said what was going on within him, not even himself. In order to form any idea of it, we must imagine what is most violent in the presence of what is gentlest.

Even in Jean Valjean's face nothing could have been seen with certainty, for it showed a sort of tired astonishment. He looked at the Bishop, that was all. But what his thoughts were would be impossible to guess.

What was evident was that he was moved and shaken. Yet what was the nature of this emotion?

He did not once glance away from the old man. The only thing clearly revealed by his attitude and face was a strange indecision. It seemed as if he were hesitating between two pits—the one that saves and the one that destroys. He was ready to dash out the Bishop's brains or kiss his hand.

After a few minutes had passed, his left arm slowly rose to his cap. This he took off. Then his arm fell again with the same slowness.

Jean Valjean renewed his contemplation. His cap remained in his left hand, his crowbar in his right, and his hair stood straight up on his savage head.

The Bishop continued to sleep peacefully beneath this terrifying glance.

A moonbeam made the cross over the mantelpiece dimly visible. It seemed to open its arms for both, with a blessing for one and a pardon for the other.

All at once Jean Valjean put on his cap again. Then he walked rapidly along the bed, without looking at the Bishop. He went straight to the cupboard. He raised his crowbar to force the door open. But the key was in the lock.

As he opened it, the first thing he saw was the basket with the silverware, which he seized. He hurried across the room, not caring about the noise he made.

Re-entering the chapel, he opened the window and seized the stick. Then he put the silver into his pocket, threw away the basket, and leaped into the garden. Bounding over the wall like a tiger, he fled.

The next morning at sunrise the Bishop was walking about the garden. Suddenly Madame Magloire came running toward him in a state of great alarm.

"Monseigneur! Monseigneur!" she screamed, "does Your Grandeur know where the silver basket is?"

"Yes," said the Bishop.

"The Lord be praised!" she continued. "I did not know what had become of it."

The Bishop had just picked up the basket in a flower bed. Now he handed it to Madame Magloire. "Here it is," he said.

"Well!" she said, "there is nothing in it. Where is the silverware?"

"Ah!" the Bishop replied, "it is the sliverware that troubles your mind. Well, I do not know where it is."

"Good Lord! It has been stolen. That man who came last night is the robber."

In a twinkling Madame Magloire had run to the chapel, entered the alcove, and returned to the Bishop. He was stooping down and looking sorrowfully at a herb whose stem the basket had broken. He raised himself on hearing Madame Magloire scream.

"Monseigneur, the man has gone! The silverware has been stolen!"

While exclaiming in this way, her eyes fell on a corner of the garden where there were signs of climbing. The wall covering had been torn away.

"That is the way he went! He leaped into Cochefilet Lane. Ah, what a horrible man. He has stolen our silverware!"

The Bishop remained silent for a moment. Then he raised his earnest eyes and said gently to Madame Magloire, "By the way, was that silverware ours?"

Madame Magloire was speechless. There was another **interval** of silence.

After that the Bishop continued, "Madame Magloire, I had wrongfully kept this silver. It belonged to the poor. Who was this person? Evidently a poor man."

"Good gracious!" Madame Magloire continued. "I do not care about it, nor does Mademoiselle. But we feel for Monseigneur. With what will Monseigneur eat now?"

The Bishop looked at her in amazement. "Why, are there no pewter[9] forks to be had?"

Madame Magloire shrugged her shoulders. "Pewter smells!"

"Then iron?"

Madame Magloire frowned. "Iron tastes."

"Well, then," said the Bishop, "wood!"

A few minutes later he was breakfasting at the same table where Jean Valjean had sat the previous evening. The Bishop gaily remarked that spoon and fork—even of wood—are not required to dip a piece of bread in a cup of milk. His sister said nothing. Madame Magloire growled in a low voice.

"What an idea!" Madame Magloire said as she went back and forth. "To receive a man like that and lodge him by one's side. And what a blessing it is that he only stole! Oh, Lord! The mere thought makes a body shake."

As the brother and sister were leaving the table, there was a knock at the door.

"Come in," said the Bishop.

The door opened and a strange and violent group appeared on the threshold. Three men were holding a fourth by the collar. The three men were gendarmes.[10] The fourth was Jean Valjean.

The corporal in charge of the group came in and walked up to the Bishop with a military salute.

"Monseigneur," he said.

At this word Jean Valjean, who was gloomy and crushed, raised his head with a dazed air.

"Monseigneur," he muttered. "Then he is not the curé."

"Silence!" said a gendarme. "This gentleman is Monseigneur the Bishop."

In the meanwhile the Bishop had advanced as rapidly as his great age permitted.

---

[9]Pewter is a material made of tin and lead or another metal.

[10]Gendarmes are French police officers.

"Ah! there you are," he said, looking at Jean Valjean. "I am glad to see you. Why, I gave you the candlesticks, too, which are also of silver and will fetch you 200 francs. Why did you not take them away with the rest of the silverware?"

Jean Valjean opened his eyes. He looked at the Bishop with an expression which no human language could translate.

"Monseigneur," the corporal said, "what this man told us was true then? We met him. Since he looked as if he were running away, we arrested him. He had this silverware—"

"And he told you," the Bishop interrupted with a smile, "that it was given to him by an old priest at whose house he passed the night? I see it all. And you brought him back here? This has been a mistake."

"In that case," the corporal continued, "we can let him go?"

"Of course," the Bishop answered.

The gendarmes loosened their hold of Jean Valjean, who tottered backward.

"Is it true that I am at liberty?" he said. He spoke in an almost **inarticulate** voice and as if in his sleep.

"Yes, you have been freed. Don't you understand?" said a gendarme.

"My friend," the Bishop continued, "before you go, take your candlesticks."

He went to the mantelpiece, fetched the two candlesticks, and handed them to Jean Valjean. The two women watched him do so without a word. They made no sign that might disturb the Bishop. Jean Valjean was trembling in all his limbs. He took the candlesticks mechanically and with wandering looks.

"Now," said the Bishop, "go in peace. By the way, when you return, my friend, it is unnecessary to pass through the front garden. You can always enter, day and night, by the front door. It is only latched."

Then turning to the gendarmes, he said, "Gentlemen, you can leave."

They did so. Jean Valjean looked as if he were on the point of fainting. The Bishop walked up to him and said in a loud voice, "Never forget that you have promised me to use this money to become an honest man."

Jean Valjean, who had no memory of having promised anything, stood silent. The Bishop, who had stressed these words, continued solemnly, "Jean Valjean, my brother, you no longer belong to evil but to good. I have bought your soul. I withdraw it from black thoughts and the spirit of damnation and give it to God."

"The Bishop's Candlesticks" was first published in 1862.

INSIGHTS INTO VICTOR HUGO

(1802-1885)

Hugo was born in Besancon, France.

Hugo actually noted that he wanted his poems to be read before an open fire. He said wine and cheese added to the mood. And Hugo, being Hugo, insisted the wine be mellow and the cheese ripe.

On Hugo's wedding day, his brother Eugene went insane. It was said that Eugene was deeply jealous of his brother's marriage. Eugene spent the rest of his life in an asylum.

Hugo was never able to shake off the guilt he felt about Eugene. That guilt worked its way into his stories. Hugo often wrote about brothers who were enemies and rivals.

The death of his favorite daughter in 1843 deeply shocked Hugo. He was so affected that he did not publish anything again until 1856.

Hugo had one unbreakable rule. He was *never* to be disturbed while he was working. No emergency was too great, no crisis too big to excuse an interruption.

His sons even joked about what would happen if a fire broke out. They teased that Hugo would not be aware of it until the flames swept over him and his manuscript.

Every morning, Hugo took a cold shower in the nude on his sundeck. This deck was in full view of anyone who cared to watch.

Word spread of Hugo's shower routine. Tourists began including it as one of their stops.

continued

But Hugo was totally unconcerned about the gawkers. He said the tourists were free people and it was their right to go where they pleased. And it was his right, he added, "to bathe where I please on my own property."

For months Hugo was obsessed by table tipping (an early version of the Ouiji board). He would summon up spirit after spirit to talk to them.

At first the whole family was caught up in Hugo's hobby. But as his interest grew more intense, the others quit playing.

Table tipping took over Hugo's life. He stopped writing. He barely ate. He didn't even keep appointments with his long-time mistress. Only the urgent need to earn a living finally forced Hugo to give up the hobby.

Other works by Hugo:
The Hunchback of Notre Dame, book
Les Miserables, book
Toilers of the Sea, book
Cromwell, play